THE STARMAN and Me

# THE STARMAN and Me

## SHARON COHEN

Quercus

QUERCUS CHILDREN'S BOOKS

First published in Great Britain in 2017 by Hodder and Stoughton

1 3 5 7 9 10 8 6 4 2

Text copyright © Sharon Cohen, 2017

The moral rights of the author and illustrator have been asserted.

A CIP catalogue record for this book
is available from the British Library.

ISBN 978 1 786 54008 9

Typeset in Sabon MT by Hewer Text UK Ltd, Edinburgh
Printed and bound in Great Britain by
Clays Ltd, St Ives plc

The paper and board used in this book
are made from wood from responsible sources.

Quercus Children's Books
An imprint of
Hachette Children's Group
Part of Hodder and Stoughton
Carmelite House
Embankment
EC4Y 0DZ

UK Company
hette.co.uk

childrens.co.uk

To Mum, Dad and my brother. My roots and my champions.
To my children. My inspirations and my future.
To Mama. Trailblazer extraordinaire.
Finally, to my husband. My love. My life.

'Somewhere, deep in the jungle,
are living some little men and women.
They are our past
and maybe,
maybe they are
our future.'
*Deep Forest*

# part one

# 1

I first saw him on the supermarket roundabout. I was in the car with Mum and Dad and we were edging into a stream of traffic when I spotted him crawling over the mound of grass.

'Go round again,' I said.

'What?'

'Go round again. There's something on the roundabout.'

Dad huffed as we circled a second time. We strained at the windows to see.

'What was it, Kofi?' said Mum. 'I can't see anything.'

'It was small and dark,' I said.

I spotted him on a bed of loose soil. He was curled into a tight ball.

'Look. There!' We slowed, but the cars behind us honked their horns and flashed their lights.

'Again, Dad! Please,' I said.

'Go on, George,' said Mum.

Dad heaved a sigh and swung the car round once more.

'Look. There at the edge,' I said.

But in that moment, he vanished.

Mum shook her head.

'Can't see a thing. Probably a silly dog or cat that's got itself stuck. Go back after tea and see if it's still there.'

I did go back. I wheeled my bike on to the pavement and watched for any movement, any sign of life. Cars and trucks rumbled by. Tall grasses dipped and swayed. Daffodils bobbed their yellow heads. I watched and waited. I fixed the image of him in my mind – deep, deep brown, all curled up, camouflaged by the soil. He didn't want to be seen, so what was he doing here?

There was a gap in the traffic. I abandoned my bike and charged across two lanes to the roundabout. A red-faced man yelled from his BMW.

'Flaming idiot!'

I clambered over the flower beds. I thrust my hands in my pockets and gazed down, trying to look like I'd lost something. There were patches of daisies, clumps of buttercups and small thistly weeds. Feathery parachutes shot upwards in the draught from the road. I found the place where I'd seen him and pressed the warm soil. I tapped the grass, hoping to feel something. I stayed there until the stream of evening commuters had petered out, until it was too dark to tell pansies from primroses, then crossed to the pavement again and cycled back up Flores Road.

Mum was wrong about it being a dog or a cat. Or any other injured animal.

Because I'd seen him.

I'd actually seen him.

And he had hands

and feet

and hair.

## 2

Saturday. 9:30 a.m.

Dad had left early for the university and Mum was heading off for morning surgery. I heard her take her keys from the hall table. She called up to me.

'One hour on the computer. And no games. Do you hear?'

'One hour, OK.'

'Get some organic oats for breakfast. With bananas. You're looking peaky.'

'Peaky, yeah, OK.'

'I'm off now. You'll have to come and lock the front door and put the chain on.'

I gathered my pyjamas and padded downstairs.

'I've left you some money for that computer magazine you wanted from Mr Barty's, but come straight home and no opening the door to anyone.'

I watched the car backing down the drive. It moved off in a cloud of exhaust. I took a bowl of oats and a cup of tea upstairs. Organic. Pure peppermint.

I switched on my computer, punched in the password and was about to start a chat with Janie when I remembered she was never up before ten on a weekend.

Then a message appeared.

`I's needin help. I's Rorty Thrutch`

**Are you from Landlow?**

`I's Rorty Thrutch`

**I don't know you. How did you get my address?**

`I's talkin to computer`

I sat back. Mum had warned me about people like this. Raving Nutters she called them.

**Sorry, but I'm not allowed to chat to people I don't know. I have to sign off**

I was about to click Block when another message popped up.

`I's needin help. I's on roundinbout at Mr Barty's`

Roundabout? My mind raced back to the thing I saw the day before. But that was on the Tesco roundabout, not the one next to the newsagent's.

**I don't think you can be at Mr Barty's because there's no signal there**

`I's on roundinbout at Mr Barty's. I's havin good signal. I's needin help`

My heart started to thump and as I right-clicked and highlighted Block I had another thought.

**Is that you Dad? Are you checking up on me?**

`I's Rorty Thrutch`

`I's needin help`

`I's on roundinbout at Mr Barty's`

**Then how are you sending me messages?**

I didn't wait for a reply. I clicked Block and logged out. I decided Mr Rorty Thrutch must be using some sort of mind-reading technology and I rushed downstairs for the aluminium foil and tore it into three sheets and moulded them to the exact shape of my head.

No gaps.


Mum says that if you're scared of something the best thing to do is to face up to it straightaway. So that's what I did.

To get to Mr Barty's you turn right at the end of the drive, take seventy-nine paces, turn right at an angle of forty-five degrees, then twelve more paces and you're in front of the shop. It was 10:24. I tugged my sweatshirt hood over my foil hat. If I needed to, I could be inside the shop in two strides, so I reckoned it was safe to turn around and see exactly what was on the roundabout at Mr Barty's.

It was one of those small ones you find at the end of Closes and Avenues that you'd probably drive over if it weren't for the hedge. It was decorated with crushed cigarette packets, empty cans and sweet wrappers. But there was no sign of a Raving Nutter. No sign of anyone at all.

I stepped into the shop. Mr Barty spotted the Hat straightaway. He scratched his turban and I felt a rush of heat to my face.

'Must have got left over from wrapping the jacket potatoes,' I said. I pulled the foil from under my hood and scrunched it into a ball.

Mr Barty smiled and lifted a bin from behind the counter. I took the shot, but it fell wide.

'Haven't seen your dad for a while,' he said. 'Still working on those techno-gadgets, is he?' He bent and scooped the ball from the floor.

I nodded.

'Mum working today?'

I nodded again. 'OK if I look at the magazines?' I said.

'No problem,' said Mr Barty and he disappeared into the back room.

I pulled *Computer Monthly* from the shelf and perched on my usual stool. I leaned back on the window and as I flicked to this week's feature article, I noticed a string of tiny letters oozing out of the page. I blinked hard and stretched my eyes. The letters were forming as if someone was writing them, one by one, from left to right.

```
I's Rorty Thrutch. I's needin help
```

I slapped the magazine closed and shoved it back on the shelf.

'I'm off, Mr Barty!'

I was through the door before he had time to reply. I leapt down the steps and was about to turn for home when I found myself dashing across the road and hurdling the gate at number 37. I lay flat on the ground. It smelt of damp earth and cat pee.

I could see the roundabout through the gap in the fence. The sky darkened suddenly and a gusty wind came rattling through the trees. It swirled the litter along the road, scooping up papers and tossing them in the air. A wrapper floated towards me, gently looped the loop, drifted over the fence and landed beside me.

Something was written inside.

```
I's not damage. I's in roundinbout
hedge. Soon I's be Bad Dead.
```

Dad came back at lunchtime with a big smile on his face.

'Great results from MINDLINK this morning. We got it working with wi-fi and managed to move a wheelchair round the room.'

'Were you sitting in it?' I said.

'Actually, I was,' he said.

MINDLINK is Dad's amazing invention. It's a brain implant for people who can't use their arms or legs. When he's finished all the tests, they'll be able to control light switches and televisions and computers just by thinking about them, *and* their own wheelchairs, apparently.

'By the way, were you on chat this morning?'

Dad shook his head. 'Far too busy. Why?'

'I got a message but I couldn't tell who it was from.'

'One of your friends?'

'Doubt it,' I said. 'Unless they're playing some sort of a joke.'

I wondered if I should tell him about Rorty. About the vanishing and the floating sweet wrapper and the weird writing on the magazine. There might have been a very good explanation for all of those things happening in the last two days, but I hadn't worked out what it could be. On the other hand, if I told Dad, he'd tell Mum and she'd probably cover me in bubble wrap and never let me out of the house again.

Maybe I should tell Janie first.

# 3

'I'm not supposed to open the door,' I said through the letterbox.

'But it's me, you idiot. You can see it's me.'

Sunday. 3:15 p.m. Janie.

I wanted to ask her if she was an alien disguised to look and sound like Janie Watts, but she was growing impatient so I didn't push it.

I said, 'I promised Mum.'

'D'you think Mumsie-dear would mind me climbing in through the window then?' she said.

I went to the lounge, slid a couple of ornaments to the side, unlocked the safety catch and let her in. She shoved her bag through first then jumped up on the sill.

'What d'you call that?' she said, staring at the Hat Mark II. Five layers of foil with spinal protection flaps.

'You don't want to know,' I said.

'One of your dad's prototypes?'

'Made it myself.'

'What's it for?'

'I don't want to say. You'll think it's daft.'

She eased herself on to the carpet.

'No I won't,' she said.

'It reduces radio-frequency electromagnetic radiation and blocks brain scanning and mind-reading possibilities from paranormal sources.'

She glared.

'Stops aliens getting into my head.'

Janie huffed. 'Bonkers, that's what you are. What would aliens find in *your* head that's so interesting?'

I brought cake and smoothies. Janie plonked herself on the sofa.

'So go on then,' she said, 'what's been going on?'

I shrugged.

'Where did you see these aliens?' She nibbled the carrot cake.

'Mum made that,' I said. 'Chock full of cardio-friendly high-density lipids, honey from ozone-free bees and carrots raised on yoghurt and rabbit droppings.'

She giggled. 'Stop changing the subject.'

'What subject?'

'The Aliens.'

'There's only one,' I said.

'There's never only one of something. Where did you see it?'

'First time was on the Tesco roundabout.'

She thought a while. 'What did it look like?'

'A bit like us, I suppose. But smaller, darker and more hairy. I think he's called Rorty Thrutch.'

She stared at me. She shook her head.

'Look. Here's proof. He sent me this.' I showed her the chocolate wrapper. 'Actually it sort of found me. It floated into Mr Gupta's front garden. This time he was on the roundabout at Mr Barty's. He seems to have a thing about roundabouts.'

Janie read the message. 'The writing's weird,' she said. 'And what does it mean *Bad Dead*?'

I shrugged. 'I've no idea.'

'You know what?' said Janie. 'I reckon this is from El Blobbo and Associates. They're always picking on kids who're not like them. They're trying to scare you.'

El Blobbo was Sebastien Fitzgerald, Sumo to everyone else. He was large, and by that I mean a roundish wobbly mass of reducing-your-lifespan adipose tissue.

He was also stupid, and by that I mean possessing the IQ of a domestic turkey.

'To be honest,' said Janie, 'the only option left for you is to drink poison. I'll try it first.'

She took a sip of Mum's smoothie. She sucked in her cheeks and stared at the pale green liquid. 'What's in it this time?'

'Yam, Ugli, Carrots and Kiwi.'

She laughed. 'Lives up to its acronym then. Don't tell your mum I said that, will you?' Her phone buzzed. She glanced at the message. 'Sorry, got to go. Should I climb back through the window or am I allowed to leave by the normal route?'

I stood at the front door and watched her skip down the drive. She turned to wave.

'Watch out for Sumo,' she called. 'He'll be after you tomorrow.'

# 4

Monday. 8:07 a.m.

Grey light filtered through the curtains. There was a cold cup of tea on the floor by my bed. My clothes were laid out on a chair and on top of them was a note from Dad, written in Twi.

*Ma wo ho nye den. Bo mmoden yiye. Ye do wo.*

It meant, *Be strong. Do your best. We love you.*

I sat on the bed with my head in my hands. I felt too sick for breakfast.

The whole night my head had been churning with visions of hairy aliens. I couldn't figure out how it was possible to vanish and make writing appear from nowhere. Either those things had actually happened or I had a horrible brain disease that was making me hallucinate. Maybe the only thing I could do was design some new headgear with ultra-maximum signal protection. And hope for the best.

The Hat Mark III comprised sixty-three centimetres of foil, shiny side out, with ear mufflers and a forehead band. I fitted it to my head, stretched a balaclava over the top and headed out of the door.

I was halfway up the hill when they got me. Stealth arrived first. He must have sprinted up the other side and crossed at the last minute. I didn't hear him coming but he hadn't earned his nickname for nothing.

I kept my head down, continued walking, lengthened my stride.

'Gi'yus yer bag,' he said. He wasn't even out of breath.

He slipped in front and lashed out, trying to knock the straps from my shoulders. He walked backwards in front of me.

'Not gorrit yet?' The voice came from behind. It was Hammer.

'Look at Mr Dafty-pants! What's that on y'head? What y'doin? Cooking brains for lunch?' He let out a sharp bark of laughter.

I tried to dodge Stealth. Swerved round him one way. He blocked. Tried the other. He blocked again.

'We just wanna 'elp ya,' whined Hammer. 'All that homey-womey work must be so heavy-weavy.'

We weren't far from school. I could have tried to run for it but Stealth was the fastest in my class, fastest in the whole school. I wouldn't have stood a chance. Hammer came in from one side and Stealth from the other and they marched me back down the road to where Sumo was waiting.

He was a year older than me but he'd failed Year 8 the first time round. He had a great moon face and dark eyes that peered out from little hoods of skin. His dad was from the Far East but had cleared off years ago. That was the story, but no one knew for sure because no one dared ask.

'Nice to see ya,' he said.

I held his gaze. I felt my eyelid twitching. He took hold of my jacket and drew me in.

'Just wanted to say hello,' he said. 'You know, walk up to school together.'

'No you didn't,' I said.

'Hammer'll carry your bag for ya.'

'No he won't.'

'We reckon it needs a bit of a sorting.'

'You can't do that. There's homework in there I've got to hand in.'

I twisted, tried to pull away, but Stealth ripped the bag from my shoulders. He tossed it in the air, caught it again and took off with it up the hill. When he reached the top he skipped across the road on to the roundabout. He unzipped the bag, opened my pencil case, turned them both upside down and started to spin. Files, books, pencils and paper spilled out in an arc over the grass.

'Why?' I yelled. I was fuming.

Sumo shrugged. 'Just a bit o'fun.'

And the three of them scarpered, shrieking and howling towards school.

If you saw your maths book sliding over the ground you'd look for strings, right? You'd think someone was playing a trick. You'd look for magnets or wires or an aerial because books just don't move on their own.

So that's what I did. I pounced on the book and frisked it. No magnets. No aerial. No bits of elastic. I listened for Hammer and Stealth. I scanned the trees and hedges and houses for Sumo working a remote control.

Then I thought, *What an idiot*. How would they have

had time to set all that up, with my stuff that'd been in my bag at home until fifteen minutes ago?

*Wally*.

There was my ruler, set square and protractor weaving in and out of the grass stems. I watched them slip effortlessly back into my bag. I closed my eyes, took a deep slow breath, then opened them again.

From the far edge of the roundabout came my calculator, sliding and scraping over the dry earth and stones, followed by my pens and pencils, wriggling like stiff little snakes. One by one they hopped into my pencil case. The zip closed and the pencil case glided over a patch of daisies back into my bag.

I stood over them gawping like an idiot.

My legs were shaking. I felt like throwing up. I bent to pick up my bag half expecting it to do a somersault. But something worse happened. I heard a voice.

'I's needin help.'

I turned.

'I's needin black holes.'

'Who is this?'

'I's needin black holes.'

'Sumo? Hammer? If this is some kind of sick joke then you can leave me alone, it's not funny any more.'

The grass whispered and shivered. A blackbird twittered in a nearby hedge.

Then another voice. 'Hey! What y'doing?'

A car was circling. It passed for a second time. It was Janie. She was waving, almost falling out of the car window.

'What y'doing you idiot?'

'Nothing,' I yelled. 'I mean something. I don't know.'

'Get a move on. It's nearly nine.'

Someone beeped and Janie's car took off again towards school.

'I have to go,' I said.

'I's needin help.'

'But I can't see you.'

'I's needin help.'

'Are you an alien?'

'Soon I's be Bad Dead.'

The voice was pleading.

'Are you ill?'

'I's needin black holes.'

'I don't understand.'

'Soon I's be Bad Dead. I's needin black holes.'

I gazed at the space around me, at the cars slowing and the kids pointing and staring. Staring at me standing there talking to myself. I drew in a deep breath and thought, *The best thing is to agree. Just agree and it'll leave you alone.*

'I'll be back at twelve,' I said.

'School Bag roundinbout?'

'Yes, I'll come back here, to School Bag roundabout, at midday, twelve o'clock. So stay here. I'll be back. I'll help with the black holes. I promise.'

5

I couldn't think. I couldn't concentrate. Mr Thompson, aka Beaky, was squeaking red brackets and multiplication signs on the whiteboard. He set us exercises on quadratic equations, which were usually dead easy, but I just couldn't do them. I couldn't focus.

I took out my phone under the desk and googled 'Black Hole'.

*Astronomy – a region of space having a gravitational field so intense that no matter or radiation can escape.*

It didn't help. I nudged Hep in the seat next to me.

'Why would someone need a black hole?' I whispered.

Hep leaned over. He grinned. He shook his head as if it was obvious. 'Because they're hungry?'

Hep was always hungry. And he always reeked. Today it was stale onions and cheese.

'Who wants one?' he whispered.

'One what?'

'A black hole.'

I paused. 'I don't know exactly.'

I looked up his name.

Rorty: *boisterous and high-spirited*

Thrutch: *narrow gorge or ravine*

None of it made sense.

Beaky handed out homework sheets and we shuffled out.

'What d'you mean hungry?' I said to Hep.

'You eat black holes when you're hungry.' Hep reached into his pocket. He pulled out a packet, shiny black with silver stars.

'They're Olioze,' I said.

Hep shook his head. 'Haven't you seen the advert? Astronomic appetite? Intergalactic hunger? You need something dark, dense and delicious. Olioze. Nothing fills you up like a Black Hole.' He made his voice go deep and echoey at the end. He took a black biscuit from the packet, punched out its thin chocolate centre and spun it around his finger.

'Black hole,' he said.

I grinned. I thumped him on the back. 'Hep. You're a genius.'

It had gone twelve. I sprinted across the playground, through the gates, and ran full pelt down the road. At School Bag roundabout, I yelled that I'd be back in three minutes with enough Black Holes to fill a Black Hole. I bought six boxes.

'I'll have to tell your mum about this,' said Mr Barty. He was hiding a smile. 'Lunch?'

'Intergalactic hunger,' I said.

The smile escaped and curled round his lips. He put the boxes in a Mr Barty's bag and I rushed out again.

It was thirteen past when I crossed the road to the roundabout. The air was still. Not a breath of wind. I spotted my pencil sharpener amongst the dandelions.

I opened the plastic bag and laid out the boxes side by side.

'Are these what you wanted?' I said. I listened for him. I waited. 'Look. I've brought Black Holes.'

I watched, willing something to move. I crawled, sweeping my hands over the grass, but I couldn't feel him.

'Are you here, Rorty Thrutch?'

No response.

'Maybe I was hearing things,' I whispered. 'Maybe it was Sumo after all. But in case you are here and I wasn't hallucinating, please help yourself. Six boxes. Twenty Olioze per box. That's one hundred and twenty Black Holes. Should keep you going for a bit.'

# 6

Four days passed. I heard nothing. I visited School Bag roundabout eight times. The boxes had gone but I couldn't be sure it was Rorty Thrutch who'd taken them. You have to respond in a humanitarian crisis, don't you? Even if you're not sure it's a human you're dealing with. Anyway, if I did nothing, very soon he'd be Bad Dead. Whatever that meant.

So I kept looking. I checked my chat messages morning and evening. I started to hang around Mr Barty's in case he'd written a little note somewhere – on the wheelie bin maybe, or on the window. I really wanted to tell Janie that I'd talked to him and he had a name and he was starving and needed help. But I had to *see* him again first. I had to be certain he was real.

Mr Barty stood in the doorway.

'Everything all right, Kofi?'

'Yeah, yeah. Just . . . you know.'

He winked.

'Waiting for a girlfriend?'

'No. No I am absolutely not,' I said.


Sunday afternoon I cycled to the ring road. If Rorty Thrutch was anywhere he'd be on a roundabout, so I started at the Tesco where I'd seen him the first time.

'Ror-tee! Are you there, Rorty?'

I waited.

Nothing.

*You big dafty*, I thought. *How's yelling going to help?*

The traffic wasn't bad so I rode around the island and mounted the kerb. I rested my bike against the blue one-way sign. I took some paper from my bag and wrote:

*Dear Mr Rorty Thrutch. Did you get the Black Holes? Send me a message if you are here. This is the roundinbout where I saw you the first time. It is near a big place that sells food and other stuff. It's called the Tesc-O.*

The big 'O', of course, is the roundabout.

I left the note in the middle with a stone on top then pedalled down Hadar Way to the next roundabout near the university. I left him notes on every single roundabout, with Rorty's voice playing over and over in my head.

I's needin help.

I's needin help.

Soon I's be Bad Dead.

Soon I's be Bad Dead.

*Maybe he really is dying*, I thought. *Maybe it's all over now and I'm too late.*

'You're soaked,' said Mum.

'It's raining.'

'Where've you been?'

'On my bike.'

She looked at me. She waited.

'Studying roundabouts,' I said.

'And does it help to have aluminium foil on your head when you're studying roundabouts?' She sighed. 'Run upstairs and get dried off, I've something to show you.'

When I came down she was holding a Mr Barty's bag.

'Where did you get that?' I said.

'Found it on the doorstep. Do you know anything about it?'

My heart was thudding. I looked inside. It was full of empty wrappers, shiny black with silver stars. Mum picked out a scrap of paper and unfolded it. She extended her arm to focus.

'My goodness, what appalling English.' She read out the message: 'I's . . . in . . . Burrows.'

I made a start for the back door. She grabbed my arm.

'Just a flipping minute,' she said. 'Who's this from?'

'I'm not sure.'

'And what on earth is Burrows?'

'You know, Burrows farm, Burrows fields, Burrows wood. The Burrows. Behind our house.'

She stared. 'So you're dashing out of the back door into . . . the Burrows . . . full of cow pats, stinging nettles and quite possibly raging bulls, in the dark and in the rain, looking for some illiterate you're not sure about?'

I pressed my lips together. 'Does seem a bit silly, doesn't it?' But in my head I was already racing down the garden to Burrows fields.

I helped her set the table.

'Dad wants to talk to you when he gets back,' she said.

'What about?'

'Well, apart from anything else you're costing us a fortune in kitchen foil.'


I was already in bed. Dad came softly up the stairs and peeped around the door.

'Still awake?' he whispered.

'Yeah,' I said.

He shifted my books and perched on the side.

'How's it going?' His voice was soft and warm, like he was wrapping me in a blanket.

'OK,' I said.

'Not too uncomfortable sleeping in a foil hat?'

'Quite warm actually. It has ear mufflers and a forehead band.'

'I can see that,' said Dad. He smiled. 'I'm supposed to ask why your school bag was ripped.'

'Sumo and that lot messing about,' I said.

'Nothing nasty then? Nothing you can't handle?'

'No,' I said.

Dad nodded.

'Then there's the biscuit wrappers,' he said. He was pressing his lips together, trying to stop himself from grinning.

I smiled. 'Nothing to worry about there either.'

'Excellent,' said Dad. 'They've been tested, you know, foil hats, in controlled experiments. Pritchard and Fynes, 2013. I'll send you the link.'

He stood up and moved to the door.

'Aren't you supposed to ask about the Burrows?' I said.

'Oh yes, almost forgot that one. If you do go, just take care.'

I smiled. 'Thanks Dad, I will.'

'Excellent. Glad that's all sorted then. Sleep well, Kofi. *Da yie.*'

'Goodnight, Dad.'

# 7

Later, when they'd gone to bed, when the lights were out, when the traffic had stopped droning and the moon lit up the dark, dark night, I crept outside and over the garden to the edge of the Burrows.

The world stood still and silent. A fine rain spattered down.

I smoothed the Hat Mark IV over my temples, clicked on the torch and stepped into the shuddering pool of light.

Burrows land stretches for miles. Acres of woods and hedges and hills and streams. I climbed a pile of old building blocks and stared out into the blackness.

'I'm here,' I whispered.

I guided the torchlight through the trees. I listened to the night breathing.

'I'm glad you liked the Black Holes. I left messages for you. On the roundabouts.'

There was scuffling in the grasses. Little creaks. Little snuffles and groans. I clambered down the rubble.

'I hope you're wrapped up warm somewhere. It's cold tonight. Cold and drizzly.'

A breeze picked up. I imagined strange creatures roaming the darkness. Heard whispery breaths and moans.

'It's late now. I should be going in.'

I took a few steps backwards and peered into the dark again.

'Keep warm, Rorty Thrutch. I'll come back. Keep safe.'

I started towards the house.

'I's here.'

I turned. Saw nothing. Little steps. A few quiet little steps.

'I's here.'

'Rorty?'

I gasped. He was so close we were almost touching.

'I's bin Bad Dead.' His face was clenched and rigid. His whole body trembled.

'You're freezing.'

He was clutching a tattered blanket. He was wearing a knotted band of rags and twisted leaves around his waist.

'You better come inside.'

He followed me over the garden and we stopped in the shadow of the doorway. I was thinking about Mum's rule of never letting strangers in the house, but Rorty was standing there, wet and shivering.

'I's bin frighted in dark dark night. I's bin Bad Dead.'

'Come on,' I said. 'Come inside where it's warm.'

He stepped on to the tiled floor and I closed the door behind him. He was tiny, barely up to my chest. His nose was broad and his forehead sloping. His hair was a mass of twisted locks and tufts and there were bony ridges above his eyes.

He gazed up at me. He stretched to touch the Hat. I heard it crumple and he whipped his hand away. A huge grin spread across his face and he stretched again, pressing the foil with both hands.

'It's aluminium,' I whispered, 'for wrapping potatoes and fish and meat. To cook them.'

His eyes creased. He started to laugh.

'Shh, we have to be quiet. My parents are asleep.'

'Shh,' said Rorty.

I took sliced ham and water from the fridge. I gave him bread and apples. We tiptoed through the hallway and up the stairs. He touched the carpet and the walls as we passed. He peered at photographs and paintings. His eyes were wide and gleaming.

I took the blanket from my bed and wrapped it around him. I gave him a bobble hat and my dressing gown to cover his feet.

'How did you find me?' I breathed.

His brow furrowed. He gave a deep sigh.

'It was you on the roundabouts, wasn't it? The one near Tesco's and Mr Barty's?'

He made a hollow click with his tongue.

'And it was you who wrote on the magazine and the sweet wrapper and put the stuff in my school bag?'

He clicked again.

'How did you disappear?'

'I's clickin an drawin an pointin an clickin.'

I imitated him. I held the tip of my tongue to the roof of my mouth and sucked down. It made a dull pop.

Rorty chuckled.

'And moving things? That scared the pants off me.'

He pointed at my headphones. He made a sharp popping sound and the cables twitched. They started to shift jaggedly over the carpet, they edged over my trainer, up my bare leg and rested motionless on my lap. My hands were shaking.

'Can you teach me how to do that?' I said.

'I's not knowin,' said Rorty. 'I's thinkin teeny thinkins an is movin.'

'Where's your home?' I said. 'Where do you come from?'

Rorty turned and stared.

'I's from green place. Many, many greens in misty misty clouds an seas of hushness. Is Forest. Is Father an Mother. I's Forest. Forest is I.'


After we'd eaten, I just sat there gazing at him. He wasn't an alien, I was sure of that. It was more like he'd walked in through an ancient door from the past – the sort of thing you'd see in a *National Geographic* magazine or in the Natural History Museum. Except he was here, in my bedroom, and his misty forest was somewhere real on Planet Earth.

Rorty looked up suddenly. His eyes were round and full of fear.

'Is not tellin,' he said. 'Kofi not tellin bout Rorty.'

'No,' I said. 'Not right now. Later maybe, when you feel safe again.'

But as I tucked the blanket around him and his eyes closed, a whole new set of worries poured into my head.

*What if he's dangerous?* Had I thought of that?

No.

Had I considered why he'd asked for my help? Me specifically?

No.

Had I invited him inside my house to look after him?

Yes.

Why did I do that?

I had no flipping idea.

I slipped out of bed and down to the kitchen, took a new roll of foil from the drawer and started on the Hat Mark V.

# 8

Monday again with our new teacher, Breeze. She pulled up the blinds and swung open the windows. She filled the classroom with air and light. She glided amongst us, skirted around benches, all bright and colourful and lovely. We sat there motionless like we were under her spell.

Her real name was Miss Ndiaye.

She said she was going to talk about Origins. She said she was going to throw ideas at us, make us think, fill our minds with wonder. Where do we come from? How did we get here?

'Each and every one of us started life as a tiny mass of cells,' she said.

She showed us a picture of a human egg, and a model of our DNA. 'This is our genetic code. It is these genes that make us unique. Our genes come from our parents, and in turn, from their parents, and their parents, and so on.'

I thought of Dad from Ghana and Mum from England. I imagined their genes combining inside a tiny ovum. Genes for dark skin and pale skin, wide nose, thin nose, curly hair, straight hair, making me, a mixture of them both.

'Who has some astonishing facts about genes?' she said.

Smarty-Pants Jocelyn raised her hand. 'If you stretched out all of the DNA from one cell it would be two metres long.'

'Brilliant,' said Breeze.

Jez spoke up.

'My dad and granddad and great-granddad were all born in Pakistan, in a little village on the edge of some dusty hills. I'm the spitting image of my granddad, so I must have some of his genes in me.'

'Fantastic,' said Breeze. 'Bring in some photos.'

Hammer said he had Viking genes.

'Prove it,' said Stealth, and there was nearly a fight.

'What about you, Kofi?' She was standing right next to me. 'Any astonishing facts to share?'

41

I thought for a while, then said, 'Many people think Watson and Crick discovered DNA but what they actually worked out was its structure and without all the great scientists before them, including Rosalind Franklin, who we hardly ever hear about, they wouldn't have won the Nobel Prize.'

Breeze gave a wide smile. 'Thank you, Kofi. Wonderful. And that's exactly what we're going to do now. We're all going to make some DNA.'

The sun beamed through the window. We started to cut out long strips of coloured card. We carefully glued them together. I imagined Rorty, his bony brow, his long arms and thick, strong hands. I wondered how someone like him was possible, how his genes must have survived for thousands of years.

I leaned over to Janie. 'Why is she teaching us Origins? Miss Crowther said we'd be doing it in the summer term.'

Janie shrugged. 'Maybe she's heard how brilliant we all are.'

She shifted closer and cupped a hand round my ear. 'Any more close encounters?'

I didn't know what to say. Janie was my best friend but I'd promised Rorty I wouldn't tell anyone about him.

'Not really,' I said.

'D'you think you were imagining it then?'

'Maybe.' I felt terrible not telling her the truth.

We pieced all the strands of DNA together. Jocelyn stood on a table and we twisted them into a double helix.

Breeze clapped and beamed and the room filled with sunshine.

'She's amazing,' said Janie. 'Why can't all teachers be like her?'

'Dunno,' I said.

'She's lovely. Just perfect.'

'Yeah,' I said, 'pretty much. A real breath of fresh air.'

It was near the end of the lesson.

'Homework,' said Breeze.

There was a collective groan.

'I would like you to think about *your* origins. Which part of your personal story do you want to explore? Prepare a page of writing that you can read out to the class in the next lesson.'

She caught my arm on my way out. 'I realise there is probably a very good reason for wearing a woollen hat with foil underneath,' she whispered, 'but our wonderful headmaster, Mr Steele, may have another opinion, so if I were you I would remove it before he sees you.'

I looked at her. Sidelong.

'OK,' I whispered.

# 9

Rorty was building a hut when I got back, down by the gate at the bottom of the garden. A framework of bendy sticks had been driven into the ground and tied with lengths of vine to form a dome. He'd gathered leaves, huge heart-shaped things with giant stems, which he was laying over the lattice. I watched as he slit the stalks and hooked them on like clothes pegs.

'Where on earth did you get those?' I said.

He turned and a smile spread across his face.

'The only place you find leaves like that is the Rainforest Biome at the Eden Project. Or the tropical house at Beads Botanic Gardens.'

Rorty's grin grew wider.

'I's likin hot leafy garden house,' he said.

He ducked low through the entrance and I followed on hands and knees. I squatted under the canopy of green. Sunlight streamed in. The earth felt warm beneath us. Rorty pushed his fingers through the frame and tugged and pulled at the leaves to close the gaps.

'Does it rain where you come from?' I said.

His eyes creased. He chuckled. 'In sharps an pins. Stabbin down down from Great Dark. Is makin floodins an wettins.' He rattled his fingers over his head and followed imaginary rivulets running down his body and over the floor. He slapped his thighs. He hooted and wailed.

'I's makin fire.'

'Good idea. Let's have a nice brew. I'll get some water.'

I brought the old camping kettle with folding handle and whistling spout. Rorty took my penknife and shaved the bark from two sticks. He guided the blade down the length of one, prised it apart and laid it on the ground. He used the other stick to drill a hole and the knife again to make a notch. He rubbed the stick with both hands from top to bottom. It twirled in the little hole, spitting out hot black dust. He knocked the powder on to a handful of dry stalks, and blew until a small flame flickered into life.

We stirred in milk. Poured in sugar. Grinned at each other as we gulped it down. Black smoke spewed from skewered bread crusts. We scraped off the carbon and smothered them in thick-cut marmalade.

'There's only one thing about being here,' I said. 'You can't let anyone see you. They won't understand. If they find you, they won't leave you alone.'

Rorty licked his lips. He bit into another slice.

'If you hear or see anyone, you'll have to do the vanishing thing,' I said.

He looked up at me from under his deep brow.

'I saw you disappear on the Tesc-O. Listen, I need to ask you a serious question now. Can you read my mind?'

His eyes darted from side to side.

'Can you see what I'm thinking?'

'I's thinkin an I's doin,' he said. He grinned.

'How did you know my email address?'

'I's talkin to computer. Is simple-pimples. Is easy-peasy.'

He scrunched his face into a frown. 'I's not doin peepin,' he said.

Later, at bedtime, I imagined him in his little hut. I thought of him pointing and clicking, moving and disappearing. It was just like using a computer except Rorty was doing all those things in the real world.

How could that be possible?

I pointed at objects in my room. School books, dirty socks, a feather from my pillow. I tried to copy his clicking sound and screwed up my eyes, willing them to move.

Nothing.

*Crackers*, I told myself. *You're crackers if you think you can do that.*

I slipped into bed and pulled the covers over my head. I breathed the stuffy air. I tried to sleep but couldn't. No point trying. Trying never works. I've already tried it.

Hours later I woke up suddenly and peered out into the dark. Nothing but a smouldering glow from the fire. I put on my dressing gown and slippers, heaved the duvet from my bed, and took it downstairs and out of the back door. Wintriness washed over me. Flecks of dew spattered my ankles. I caught the scent of the fire, made my way to the hut and crawled inside.

He'd made a chair from four splayed sticks. They were tied in the middle with a thick stem. His back was resting along one and his feet were hooked over another.

I went back for woollies and draped them over his shoulders. I tucked Mum's college blanket over his legs and feet. Rorty opened one eye and smiled.

I could see he'd been painting. I shone the light on the slabs of stone. A group of little bodies in the forest. Men with spears and axes. Monkeys hanging from vines. Small horned antelope leaping through the bush. Colours of the sun and the earth and the trees and the sky. Colours of his Forest.

I settled on the floor next to him, curled up in the duvet. I listened to his gentle breath. Watched the rise and fall of his chest. Saw the deep shadow on his face below his brow.

The next thing I knew it was morning and Mum's voice was calling me. I scrabbled out on to the wet grass and sprinted for the house.

I saw her opening the back door, standing in the doorway, coming down the path towards me.

'What on earth . . .?' she said.

Her hair was all over the place and her eyes were still puffy with sleep. She looked beyond me to the hut. 'What on earth?' she said again. She felt my hands, drew the duvet round my shoulders and looked right into me. 'You didn't, did you?' she said.

'Not all night,' I said.

She pulled me inside. Sat me down. Poured tea. Spooned in honey. Watched as I drank it down.

'What's going on, Kofi?'

'I've been reading about the rainforest. It's a primitive dwelling.'

'You mean you built that thing? By yourself?'

I shrugged. I didn't want to lie.

'Primitive dwelling, my foot. You're lucky you didn't catch your death.'

She felt my head and brushed my cheek with the back of her hand. She popped a vitamin into my mouth.

'Go up and get dressed,' she said. 'I'll drive you in this morning.'

# 10

It was Wednesday, around four. We were in the hut again. I'd pulled a wicker trellis over the entrance to keep out the cold. Thunder rumbled in the distance and raindrops pattered on the roof. I'd brought him a jumper and trousers which were miles too big. I rolled up the sleeves and trimmed the trouser legs with the kitchen scissors.

'That's better,' I said. 'You'll be nice and cosy now.'

Rorty looked at me. His brow furrowed. He reached up to catch the green drips falling from my hair.

'Is rainin funny colourins,' he said.

I drew in a deep breath and blew it out again.

'It's paint,' I said. 'Sumo, Hammer, Stealth – you know, the ones on School Bag roundabout – except this time they ambushed me in the snicket that runs down by Crowlands. Sumo poured paint over my head and they've completely crushed the Mark V.'

I smoothed the crumpled foil, straightened the chinstraps and reshaped the cranial padding. Rorty pulled a blanket round my shoulders and squatted beside me. I felt his fingers pulling and tugging, felt him gently teasing the paint from my hair.

'What would you do against idiots like that, Rorty? Can you make a spear? Can you make a bow and a poisoned arrow? I'd kill them you know, if I had the chance. I'd kill the lot of them.'

He edged around me and sighed. Just his calm breath on my neck and the gentle tugging of my hair.


Later I took him baked potatoes and grilled salmon. Mum was pleased I seemed to be eating more. She piled my plate with whole roasted carrots.

'Look at those shoulders,' she said. 'Proper young man you're growing into, aren't you?'

She eyed me as I covered the plate and opened the back door. It was dark, and it was chucking it down again.

'Checking if the hut's waterproof,' I said, before she had the chance to ask.

'Wait.' She brought an umbrella from the hall cupboard. 'In case you have a leak.'

It was about eight-thirty when we heard the dog. The rain had eased and the wind had dropped to a whisper. Smoke drifted up from the fire. I shifted the trellis and looked out. Darkness had melted everything black except for the tree tips against the night sky.

'What was that?' I said.

We peered into the blackness and smelt the night air. We heard the traffic rumbling, and again, the faint yapping of a dog.

'Torches, Rorty. Look.'

Way in the distance were three bobbing lights. We crawled out. We watched the beams waver and blink.

'Is more,' said Rorty.

Coming from behind was another spot. And another.

'They're heading this way,' I whispered.

My heart was clattering, my breath steaming in the cold air.

'Please don't let it be Sumo. Can you see them, Rorty? Can you see who it is?'

We heard the thud of boots and a faint beep, beeping.

The dog was yelping frantically as it strained on its leash. We heard their voices.

'Signal's getting stronger.'

'Over there by the hedge.'

'We're on to something, Gerry.'

'Go on, Sirus. Get it, lad!'

I grabbed Rorty. 'Climb the tree, go invisible, then put on the foil Hat.'

The lights were wobbling now and something was thundering towards us through the grass.

'Climb the tree, Rorty. And disappear. Now!'

Rorty grabbed the remnants of the Hat Mark V. He sprinted for the beech tree and launched himself up the trunk. Seconds later a huge dog crashed through the roof of the hut.

Sticks snapped and branches collapsed as it landed in a frenzy of snarling and saliva. It pounced on the umbrella, snapped it up and shook it. Its great form writhed. The noise was terrifying. Its hind paws caught the edge of the dinner plate, which flicked into the air and smashed on the stones by the fire.

I curled into a ball and covered the back of my neck with my hands.

One of the men yelled, 'In here, Gerry!'

I heard leaves ripping and felt branches being yanked from the ground. A blinding light fell across my face.

'That's no flaming monkey.'

He shoved my shoulder. Rolled me over. Pulled me up by my collar. He growled at the dog.

'Enough, Sirus.'

Sirus lay down. His ribcage heaved and his great tongue flopped in his mouth.

'Where's the monkey?' Spit sprayed from his walrus moustache. Sweat glistened in the furrows of his brow. I stared. He shook me, his grip tightening.

'Tell us, kid, or you're in big trouble.'

'Are you from the zoo?' I said. Somehow I managed to sound calm but inside I was terrified.

He leaned closer. 'We got its signal. The monkey's here.'

A younger man stepped forward. 'Who made this?' he said, shining a beam at the dome. He groped at the huge leaves. 'Where are these from?'

'Sourced locally,' I replied.

'What sort of plant?'

'Genetically modified.'

I couldn't help it. It just blurted out.

He scowled. 'Genetically modified what?'

'Rhubarb. Little experiment in the greenhouse.'

Sirus growled. He'd caught another scent. He pushed through the mess and bounded over to the beech tree. The men followed, flashing their lights at its dark skeleton, staring into the night sky. Sirus stood on his hind legs and ripped at the bark.

The man with the machine fiddled with the switches. He flicked lights on and off.

'Lost it,' he said. 'Not so much as a blip.'

'What are you tracking it with?' I asked.

'None of your flaming business,' he said.

Another of the men tried to climb. He wedged a foot on a knot at the base. He reached up and scrabbled at the trunk. He groped for handholds but the branches were too high.

'Leave it,' said Gerry. 'Probably cleared off somewhere else by now. You sure you didn't see it? Biggish thing. Dark-coloured.'

'Dangerous?' I said.

'Course,' said Gerry. 'Deadly. Let us know if you catch sight of it.'

'How will I do that?'

'We'll be back,' he said.

And they took their electronic gadget and their torches, their sour smell and their big boots, and they left.

I waited at the bottom of the tree. Rorty climbed down slowly. His limbs were shaking and his teeth were chattering from the cold. I wrapped him in my coat and carried him past his broken hut and up the garden path by the hedge.

'Why were they looking for you?' I said. 'How were they picking up a signal from you?'

Rorty shivered. 'I's not knowin,' he said.

'Where were you before you found me?'

He sighed. He didn't seem to remember.

'You'll have to stay in the house now. In my room. It's not safe out here any more.'

Rorty gripped me tighter as I carried him inside.

# 11

Next day. Teatime. He'd made a little den in my room with the blanket and the stone paintings that we'd rescued from the hut. He kept trotting to the window and peeping out to check if the dog had come back.

'You're safe here,' I told him. 'They can't come inside.'

''s likin here,' he said.

Mum wasn't back and we were hungry so he made Olioze. Six boxes. He scrunched up his face, clicked his tongue and there they were. I howled as they tumbled from his hands.

'But it's absolutely, utterly impossible,' I shrieked. 'It defies the laws of physics. How d'you do it, Rorty? How?'

Rorty laughed and laughed. 'I's not knowin. I's thinkin an makin thinkins.'

Breeze hadn't been at school that morning so we'd had Velociraptor instead. We'd done the structure of matter. He'd strutted up and down, elbows glued to his sides and hands flapping as he squawked on about protons, electrons, neutrons – the stuff of all things.

*Matter can neither be created nor destroyed.*

So where had all the stuff come from to make six boxes of Olioze?

We lay on the floor in strips of sunlight, watching the dust motes swirling and blinking like miniature universes. Rorty found the Dusty Hoardings under my bed. That's Mum's name for them. He pulled out the cardboard box labelled Baby Things and brought out a tiny shoe. He tipped the box and found the other one and put his fingers inside them and made them walk across the floor. There was my umbilical clip and the tiny wristband that I'd worn in the hospital. He emptied my baby teeth from a plastic bag and arranged them in a row on the bed.

Then he brought out a small wooden chest. I told him these were my Treasures, my most precious things of all. A crocodile tooth. The tiny skull of a mouse. A four-leaf clover between sheets of blotting paper. A bumblebee wrapped in cotton wool. Tiny shells from Pentle Bay beach. He fingered each precious thing and made soft clicking sounds with his tongue.

Rorty moved closer and I felt the warmth of him next to me. I wondered for the millionth time how he'd been followed. He didn't have an electronic tag or bracelet, so how did Gerry's machine search him out?

'You know, if those men were able to track you, it's probably best if you keep the Hat on all the time,' I said.

'Kofi keepin Rorty safe from nasti men. Rorty keepin Kofi safe from nasti green paintin Sumo.'

I laughed. 'Thanks, Rorty, but don't actually shoot Sumo with poisoned arrows, will you? That's definitely not allowed.'

I left him and went down for tea. I poked at the food on my plate.

'Not hungry?' said Mum.

'Not really.'

'Heard you chattering to yourself.'

'Yeah, don't worry about that.'

I got up and took some foil from the kitchen drawer. Mum tutted and sighed.

'Trust me,' I said. 'It's important.'

I printed a Warning Notice in red, bold, ALL CAPS, Font 72 and stuck it on my bedroom door.

**KNOCK BEFORE ENTERING.
I AM 12 AND REQUIRE PRIVACY.
PLEASE WAIT FOR A POSITIVE RESPONSE
BETWEEN THE KNOCKING AND THE
ENTERING. THANK YOU.**

Then I sat down with Rorty and designed the Hat 3000 Super Series. This one was for him, of course.

# 12

Sumo had no idea his face was turning green. He was sitting opposite me in Art. When he looked up his forehead was a violent shade of lime. I watched the colour seep down his temples, curve under his eyes and spread over his cheeks and lips.

Janie saw him next. She gasped and clamped a hand to her mouth. A thin red streak slid from the centre of his hairline and motored steadily down his nose. Next, a strap of white washed over his chin and little black dots appeared, one by one, above his eyebrows. It was as if the paint was leaching through his skin.

Bit by bit the rest of the class noticed. Heads turned. Fingers pointed. There were hoots and shrieks, little yelps of surprise. The noise grew to a crescendo. Kids jostled and elbowed to take a look at him.

'Shrek!' someone yelled.

'The Hulk!'

Alice Granger squealed and shrank away. I tried not to look like I knew exactly what was happening.

Mrs Deft, who had been searching for gouges and chisels in the Art cupboard, backed out and fought her way through the bodies. Her mouth tightened as she gazed down at him.

'Absolute blooming daftness,' she said. 'The epitome of silly nonsense. I'd expect this sort of thing at primary school. And where did you get that paint?'

She searched the table. She brushed aside little slivers and shavings of soap.

'Go wash it off,' she said.

Sumo rubbed his cheek and examined his fingers.

'What paint? What y'on about?'

Mrs Deft fluttered her eyelids. She pursed her lips and pointed to the sink. Sumo raised his great bulk and kicked back the chair. The crowd parted and Mrs Deft turned on the tap and handed him a sponge.

'Soap,' we heard her saying. 'Lots and lots of soap.'

Minutes later Sumo stood up, water dripping from his nose and chin.

'No blooming difference,' said Mrs Deft, 'you're not scrubbing hard enough.' She held up a mirror. Sumo examined his face.

'What the . . .?' he said.

'How?' said Janie.

It was 4:06 p.m. We were heading home, turning into Boxgrove Drive. We'd trailed Hammer and Sumo and left them outside Mr Barty's. Sumo was peering at his reflection in the shop window. He was licking his finger and having another go at the paint. We crossed the road and sat on a wall.

'The paint was *moving*,' said Janie. 'How can paint *move*?'

I wanted to tell her. I wanted to say that he'd followed me to school and he was taking revenge on Sumo for covering me in paint. I wanted her to know that he was near us right now, that he was invisible, that the shimmering shape by the trunk of the sycamore tree was Rorty Thrutch.

But I was scared. I just wasn't sure how she'd react.

'Hope it comes off,' she said.

'Why?'

'Can you imagine what his stepdad'll do to him? He's unhinged. Raving. You've seen the bruises.'

'Serves him right,' I said. 'Anyway, it doesn't come off. Well, not with traditional methods.'

'And what do you know, Mister Flipping Picasso?'

'It won't come off with water, soap or turpentine, although sandpaper could be interesting. That sort of paint only comes off with magic.'

Janie rolled her eyes and shook her head.

I stood up and moved to the tree. I saw the edge of him, the faint curve of the 3000 Super Series on his head.

'Can you undo?' I whispered.

I heard him click.

'Are you sure?'

He clicked again. I stepped forward and fixed my eyes on Sumo.

'Hey, you!' I waved. I danced. I flopped about like an idiot. The duo turned and glared.

'Having a few problems with your make-up?'

Janie jumped up. She pulled me back.

'What are you doing?' she squealed.

Hammer came first. Shoulders hunched. Fists punching the air.

I reached out and felt the warmth of the little body by the tree.

'Steady now,' I whispered. 'Slip off the Hat and wait till I say the word.'

Sumo followed. They were gathering speed now. Crossing the road. Hammer broke into a trot.

'Getting a little agitated, are we?' I said. 'I thought you liked painting, you great pair of jerks.'

'You've lost it,' breathed Janie. 'They're going to murder you.'

They thundered up to me. I faced them. I tensed. Hammer reached out a hand and shoved me and I toppled backwards on to the pavement.

'Wait,' I said, pulling myself up again. 'No really, I think green suits you. And those black dots are gorgeous.'

'Did you do this?' said Sumo.

'Me? How could I?'

'You were sitting there when it happened.'

'With a paint brush in my hand?'

Sumo folded his arms across his chest.

'I might know how to get rid of it though,' I said.

I held out my hand. '*Mabeng se ogya!*' I shouted. '*Okukuseku! Meye deng se! Okukuseku!*'

It sounded brilliant. Like a real spell. It meant, 'I am clever and powerful, like fire! I am tough!'

I wailed high and low. Fluttered my eyelids. Turned on my heels one way, then the other way. Made a big meal of it. Then I thrust my hand towards Sumo and yelled.

'*Tu yera!*' and the paint disappeared.

Every single bit of it.

All at once.

Janie gasped.

'Jeez!' said Hammer.

'What?' said Sumo.

'It's gone.'

'All of it?'

He peered at Sumo's face. He drew a thumb across his cheek as if there might still be a trace of it. Hammer took a step back and gazed at me through narrowed eyes.

'What's going on?' he said.

I shrugged. 'Little trick.'

'Never seen no trick like that.'

'First time for everything.'

'Has it really gone?' said Sumo.

'Yeah,' said Hammer.

They turned and considered me.

I shrugged again. 'Nothing like a damn good trick,' I said.

I hooked Janie's arm. 'Come on,' and we charged down Boxgrove Drive.

'What the heck?' Janie kept saying. 'What the heck?'

I steered her across the road.

'Just keep walking. Don't look back.'

We huddled by the hedge outside my house.

'How did you do that?' Her voice was a stifled squeal.

'I can't explain now,' I whispered.

'Yes you can. How did you do that?'

'Best thing is to go home. Not sure how they'll react. Don't stop. Go home and lock the door.'

Janie glowered at me through a veil of hair. She hitched her bag on her shoulder.

'You will tell me.' She started down the road, swept round again. 'You *will* tell me, you know.'

## 13

She came round the next morning. Saturday.

'Kofi. It's Janie,' called Mum.

I heard her soft steps on the stairs. She knocked.

'Wait!' I said.

I scrabbled for undies, dragged a pair of trousers from the back of the chair. I wafted deodorant around the room.

She knocked again.

'I – am – waiting – for – the – positive – response – between – the knocking – and – the entering,' she said.

I hesitated. There'd be no going back now, she'd make me tell her everything. She'd see Rorty. She'd know about copying and disappearing and moving stuff.

'Wake up, you noodle,' she shouted.

'I'm coming.' I slipped on a T-shirt and opened the door.

She was wearing faded jeans and a white studded belt, her hair tied up in a ponytail. She was about to speak when she caught sight of the paintings. She gave a little gasp.

'Holy Moly,' she said, going over and half-kneeling in front of them.

There were circles of earthy reds. Silhouettes of birds, turtles, lizards, snakes. There were trees, tall and towering, feathery ferns, exotic flowers and in amongst them little dots of ochre and coppery brown.

'Did you —?' she started. 'No, couldn't have been. You're rubbish at painting. Who did them?'

My mouth opened, and closed again. I imagined her seeing Rorty for the first time. I saw her turning deathly white and fainting and knocking her head as she fell to the floor and me panicking and dashing downstairs to phone her mum and her mum arriving and my dad lifting her to the car and Janie staying off school for weeks and weeks and her mum saying she'd been psychologically traumatised and would never fully recover from the shock. And then I imagined her shouting at me, *You dork, You Complete Wacko! I never, ever want to see you again!* and storming out and slamming the door and her whole family emigrating.

To Australia.

'You OK?' she said.

I pulled her to the side of the room near the window.

'You better sit down,' I said.

She let her bag fall to the floor and sat cross-legged. Her bare knee poked through a tear in her jeans.

'Go on then. I'm listening.'

'There's no easy way to say this.'

We heard the beanbag rustling and a gentle clicking from under the bed.

I spoke softly. 'Rorty. Come and say hello.'

The Hat emerged first. He crawled out and sat up and rubbed his eyes. He dragged his blanket and pulled it around his shoulders. His hands and legs were covered in spots of coppery brown.

'Janie. This is Rorty Thrutch.'

She sat motionless, her eyes wide and unblinking. Rorty reached for a packet of Olioze and pushed it towards her.

She didn't move.

'It's OK,' I said.

She stretched and pulled a wrapper from the box. Shiny black with silver stars. She tore it open and put the biscuit to her lips, started to nibble round the edge. Her eyes moved from Rorty to me and back again. It was impossible to tell what she was thinking.

'I know it sounds crackers, but Rorty contacted me on chat.' I laughed. 'He needed help. He was starving and he was in danger but I've no idea why he chose me. He can do incredible things like disappearing and copying and moving stuff without touching it and writing, and then there's the painting – through his fingers.'

We looked at the row of stones. Tracings of ancient figures, like a line of little portholes into the past.

'He's from the Forest,' I said. 'But he doesn't remember where and he doesn't know why he's here.'

Janie trimmed the dark scalloped edge of the biscuit. She smiled and held out her hand.

'I'm Janie,' she said.

Rorty's brown fingers extended to hers. The pale pads brushed her palm, then stretched and enveloped it.

'I am very pleased to meet you.' She smiled again. 'I'd like another biscuit please.'

We sat a while, the three of us, munching and gazing and munching.

'Did you really paint Sumo's face?' said Janie.

'I's choosin lovely colourins. All wigglies an dotty dots.'

'And you made the paint disappear?'

'Is bestest. Is father givin im nasties an blue-skins.'

'And did you make yourself disappear?'

Rorty stared.

Janie folded the biscuit wrapper into a thin strip and tied it in a knot. She sighed and looked over at me.

'What did you mean copying and moving stuff without touching it?' She looked back at Rorty. '*How* can you disappear?'

Rorty glanced at me. I shook my head.

'Not now,' I said. 'Next time maybe.'

'No! You said that yesterday,' said Janie. 'I have witnessed paint appearing out of nowhere and I've seen that same paint disappearing. I've been up all night trying to figure it out. And now you tell me that Rorty can copy things, move them and make himself disappear and you want me to wait to find out how?'

Rorty licked his fingers. He stood up. He looked at me as if to ask if it was OK.

I shrugged and nodded.

He removed the Hat and went over to the bookcase by the far wall. He pointed to it, at the shelves, the rows of books, the piles of DVDs. He stood on tiptoes and drew a great oval in the air. He made a soft click in his throat, turned to us and pointed to himself, then gave another click, and disappeared.

We sat staring at the empty space.

I heard Janie swallow. I heard her breathing quicken.

'I's here,' said his voice.

A pale light slanted through the window. There was a shimmering, an edge of something, a vague shape flickering. I could make him out now, the edge where he didn't match the background, and when he moved the lines of him and the bookcase no longer matched up.

'Not invisible,' said Janie, 'camouflaged.'

Rorty clicked his tongue and came back.

Janie jumped and drew in a shuddering breath. She stood up. 'I-I should be going,' she whispered.

'You don't have to. Stay for breakfast. You know Mum loves—'

'I can't,' she interrupted. 'We're off somewhere soon.' She edged to the door.

'I'll show you out then,' I said.

'It was lovely to meet you, Rorty. I hope I'll see you again soon.'

'I'll be back, Rorty,' I said. 'Don't make any noise.'

Janie's ponytail bobbed as she trotted downstairs.

I opened the front door.

'I'm sorry,' I said.

'It's OK. I'm just a bit . . .'

'I know. I'll walk home with you if you like.'

We took the usual route down Boxgrove Drive, heading for the university. Janie pushed her hands in her pockets and fixed her eyes on the pavement. She seemed miles away.

We followed the path through the park. Kids on the swings yelled at us. They waved and shouted – 'Cyberman' or something – but we were too far away to hear.

We turned a corner and started up Glaston Avenue. When we reached her house, she perched on the wall, still deep in thought. Sunlight dappled her hair. She squinted up at me.

'Have to go soon,' she said.

'Don't go to Australia, will you?' I blurted.

She laughed. 'What are you talking about?'

'Dunno. I dunno.'

Her mum came out. 'So that's where you are. We're off in five minutes. Want to come, Kofi?'

I looked at Janie.

'Tesco's,' she said, pulling a face. 'Not Australia, you noodle.'

'Oh. No thanks, Mrs Watts.'

Janie's mum smiled and winked. 'Like your hat,' she said.

I'd forgotten all about it. I snatched it from my head and scrunched it into my pocket. I felt stupid.

'Did it work?' said Janie. She patted the wall for me to sit down.

'What d'you mean?'

'The Hat. Can he read your mind?'

'Oh. No. I don't think so.'

'He's not an alien, is he? Not the extra-terrestrial sort. Maybe he's from prehistoric times. Pre-*Homo sapiens*. One of our ancient, ancient ancestors.'

'That's what I thought. But how's it possible? How can he be here now? From another time? Another age?'

Janie shrugged. She sighed. We turned our eyes skyward and watched the clouds scudding and the gulls soaring.

'Someone's after him,' I said. 'He built a hut in the garden and they were tracking him with an electronic bleeping device and this massive dog landed on the hut and wrecked it. That's why he's in my room.'

'Who were they?'

'A giant walrus called Gerry. And four others. And the Hound from Hell. It would have killed him, I'm sure. We can't let them near him again.'

Janie's mum called. Janie jumped up, scraped back her hair and re-looped the elastic. She thought a while then looked at me.

'It's dead exciting this, isn't it?'

'Weird and scary,' I said.

'Wacky and wonderful,' she said.

She grinned. She started skipping towards the car.

'I'll help you rebuild the hut,' she shouted. 'Bigger and stronger. Somewhere no one will find it.'

'Better be soon,' I said. 'Before they come back again.'

# 14

She called round again on Sunday afternoon. Mum was out with the jogging club, Dad had gone to the gym and Rorty was in the shower. I ran downstairs to let her in, then ran straight upstairs again.

'Can't leave him unsupervised,' I said. 'First time he left the plug in and we nearly had a flood.'

There were squawks and shrieks coming from the bathroom. Rorty was plastered in bubbles and foam.

'Is hot rain,' he said, pointing at the shower. 'Is hot rainin rain.'

I washed him off, wrapped a towel round him and was rubbing him dry when Janie spotted something.

'Wait,' she said. She was peering at Rorty's head. She parted his damp hair gently to expose his scalp. There was a mark. A wound. A scar on the top of his head. We saw dark lines where the stitches had been.

A terrible shock ran through me. I'd seen something like this before in exactly the same place.

Janie crouched and looked deep into his eyes. 'Who did this to you?' she said.

He put his fingers to his head and felt gently along the scar. 'I's not remembrin,' he said.

We went to my room and stood by the window where it was light.

'What do you think it is?' Janie whispered.

'Craniotomy,' I said.

'What's that?'

'They make an incision, peel back the skin and remove a piece of skull.'

'What for?'

'To take something out. Or put something in.'

'How d'you know?'

I stopped. I looked straight at her.

'My dad told me.'

I asked Mum if Janie could stay for dinner. I wanted her to ask Dad about MINDLINK to find out more details about his experiments. I was supposed to join in now and again so it didn't seem like an interrogation. I still couldn't believe for one minute that Dad had been testing his technology on Rorty.

We'd finished the roast lamb and were starting on Mum's low-fat sponge when I gave Janie a nudge. She turned to Dad.

'Do you mind if I ask what you're working on?' she said. 'Kofi's been telling me and it sounds really exciting.'

'Oh, don't get him started,' said Mum. 'You'll never hear the end of it.'

Dad chuckled. 'Of course you can, Janie.' He leaned across the table. 'Imagine this. Someone who is paralysed being able to switch on the TV and the lights and the computer using only the power of their mind.'

'That's nothing, Dad,' I said, trying to keep things light. 'Imagine me sitting on the sofa with my arms folded playing *Call of Duty* using only the power of *my* mind.'

'Shh,' said Janie.

Dad went on. 'What about someone unable to move their limbs but able to move themselves in a wheelchair, just by thinking about it?'

'Is that possible?' said Janie.

'What about me, sitting in my Bugatti Veyron Super Sports, accelerating through seven speeds, doing nought to sixty in two-point-five seconds, just by thinking about it,' I said.

'Be quiet, Kofi,' said Janie. 'Let your dad speak.'

'He's too modest. It's going to be revolutionary.'

Dad shrugged. 'We don't know that. We haven't tested it in humans yet.'

I caught Janie's eye.

'Well get on with it then,' shouted Mum from the kitchen.

Dad shook his head and smiled.

'One thing's for sure,' said Mum, coming back in, 'it'll make a huge difference to people with spinal injuries.'

'Has it got a name?' said Janie.

'MINDLINK,' said Dad. 'Come on, I'll show you.'

We followed him to his study. He put on his glasses. Tapped the computer keys. A picture of a tiny black square came on-screen. There was a penny coin next to it to show how small it was.

'This is MINDLINK,' he said. 'It's a silicon chip. When it's implanted on the surface of the brain it sends signals directly to a computer. Over time MINDLINK learns the language of the brain by listening to thoughts and using those thoughts to make machines work.'

We watched a simulation video of someone playing computer ping-pong.

'When the person thinks "up",' said Dad, 'MINDLINK sends the signal to the computer and the paddle moves up. And when they think "down" the paddle moves down.'

Janie took a deep breath. 'Why haven't you tested MINDLINK in humans?' she said.

'We don't have permission just yet,' said Dad.

'Why not?' I asked.

'We think there might be a few problems with loss of memory. We have to be sure the chip is working properly first.'

'What about any other animals? You know, primate-type-things?' said Janie, waving her hands as if trying to form what she was thinking in the air.

Dad shook his head. 'Not that I know of. And I am head of the Research Group, so I *should* know.'

'So could MINDLINK be used for anything other than playing computer ping- pong?' said Janie.

Dad nodded. 'Oh yes. As I said, the goal is to help people with paralysis. When we've improved the point-and-click mechanism, MINDLINK will be able to control all sorts of devices and machines just using thoughts. In five years' time, there's no doubt we'll have mind-controlled prosthetics.'

'Robotic arms, artificial legs,' I said.

'I know what prosthetics are,' said Janie, 'but that's not what I meant. What I meant was, could MINDLINK be used for something like camouflage?'

Dad frowned. His eyes flickered.

'Or telekinesis?' said Janie. 'And I'm talking major moving-stuff-around here. Or using your thoughts to create things? Biscuit-size. Car-size. Whatever you like really. And what if you could paint with your mind? Like you just have to think of the colour, concentrate and *whoosh*, there it goes all over the place.'

'I think that's plenty of examples, Janie,' I said, elbowing her.

Dad chuckled. 'What an imagination. We could do with you on our research team.' He smiled. 'Maybe one day, Janie, but that sort of technology is far beyond what we can do right now. And far beyond what we may ever *want* to do. To develop that kind of expertise would not be without risk either. I do not want to consider the consequences of molecular replication, even if it were possible.'

'Is anyone else developing something similar to MINDLINK?' I said.

'Not really,' said Dad. 'Some researchers are using electro-caps but we're the only ones using a chip that's implanted on the surface of the brain.'

'Could anyone have stolen MINDLINK? You know, to use it for things it's not meant to be used for.'

Dad sat back in his chair and thought a while. 'I sincerely hope not, but only someone who suspects something would ask a question like that.'

He waited for me to respond but I didn't know what to say. I didn't want to give Rorty away.

'Where exactly is it put in the brain?' said Janie.

'On the motor cortex,' said Dad. He clicked on a series of diagrams. The last one showed a tiny scar at the top of the head in exactly the same place as Rorty's.

Janie sat back and we stared at each other. We were quiet for a while.

Dad cleared his throat. 'Well, if you're done, I have something to tell you. I owe you an apology, Kofi.'

'Why's that?' I said.

'I had to go into your room yesterday. Without your permission. I heard noises. Something banging and scrabbling about.'

I held my breath. I wondered if he knew.

'When I opened the door everything went quiet.'

I shrugged. 'Then, I dunno.'

'I found this.' He plucked a paper tissue from his desk and peeled it open. He pulled out a clump of black hairs. 'In the shower,' he said.

'Oh. That's interesting.'

He waited for me to elaborate.

'They're not mine,' I said.

Dad glanced at Janie. She knew what he was thinking. She shook her head.

'Bella is a *golden* retriever,' she said. 'And I promised I wouldn't wash her in your shower again. I stick to my promises, you know.'

Dad looked at us. He massaged his forehead and rubbed his eyes.

'Sorry if we've been a bother,' said Janie.

'You're no bother,' said Dad.

'And thanks for answering all our questions. Your work is really interesting.'

'My pleasure.' He stood up and moved to the door. 'Time for another piece of cake?'

'If we're lucky,' I said. 'Mum's had at least half an hour in there completely unsupervised.'

# 15

She hadn't touched the cake. She was fast asleep on the sofa. We took two pieces upstairs and Janie closed the door.

We sat cross-legged on the rug and Janie stared blankly at the wall and sighed.

'Your dad wouldn't lie to us, would he?'

'Absolutely not,' I said.

'But it's weird that Rorty's scar is exactly like the diagram he showed us.'

'Look, Janie, my dad has nothing to do with Rorty. He sticks to the rules. He wants to help people, not get himself locked up.'

'But the fact is *someone* put *something* in Rorty's head and it's very likely to be one of your dad's silicon chip thingies – so how did that happen?' She scowled.

'*And* this mysterious someone brought Rorty here from some undiscovered corner of the planet, which, by the way, is pretty much the Discovery of the Century, like Darwin's Theory of Evolution, *and* by the way also, the rest of the world doesn't know about yet otherwise it would have been in every magazine and newspaper and TV channel, *plus* this Whoever-it-is must be really smart because they've made the silicon-thingy work in ways your dad hasn't dreamt of yet.' She drew in a deep breath.

'You've really thought this through, haven't you?' I said. 'And now it seems much more serious and worrying and scary and we're right in the middle of it! But Dad didn't put MINDLINK in Rorty, I'm one hundred per cent sure of that.'

She plucked a raspberry from her cake. 'Gerry and those men won't stop looking for Rorty, you know. Not if he's as valuable as this. What if they break into the house when you're at school? He can't stay here any more, can he?'

I felt my stomach clench at the thought of it. I shook my head.

'So where's he going to live?'

'I've no idea,' I said.

She took her phone. 'Let's make a list.'

I thought a while. 'Wherever it is, it has to be dog-proof,' I said. 'Well, Sirus-proof. And isolated, but not too far away because we'll need to visit him.'

Janie tapped it in.

'Since they're tracking him with that bleeping machine, he'll have to keep wearing the Hat,' she said. 'Unless you can think of another way to stop the signal working.'

'Add that to the list. I'll have to come up with another design. Something more permanent.'

Janie pondered. 'When we take him to his new home, we'll have to carry him so there's no trace of his scent on the ground.'

I nodded. 'We'll spray him with deodorant then carry him in the rucksack.'

'He's not going to like that,' she said.

We listed other things he'd need: firewood and fresh water. A waterproof hut and warm bedding. And although he could conjure up whatever food he'd already copied, he seemed keen on fishing, so we added 'near a river'.

Janie got up. She gazed outside. Total darkness. No moon. Not even a twinkling star.

'What if he's lonely?' she said.

'Better than being splashed all over the newspapers or caught by madman Gerry.'

'But he's got no one, has he? No one like him.'

'Not that we know of. You were the one saying there's never only one of something.'

'Yeah I did, didn't I?' She came away from the window and sat on the bed. 'Make sure he feels safe, won't you? It must be so weird being here, far away from his Forest and his family. Tell him we'll look after him and find a way to take him home.'

I smiled.

'I'll tell him,' I said.


Long after Janie had gone and the house was quiet, and I knelt on my bed and gazed out into the night, I saw three floating points of light, distant and flickering, advancing slowly, disappearing, reappearing. Three shimmering cones stretching and piercing the darkness, shuddering over the Burrows, over the breeze blocks and hardened packets of cement and closing in beyond the fence.

And with them came two glowing eyes, menacing eyes, searching for Rorty Thrutch.

# 16

Monday again. We'd had Beaky for Maths and Trixie for French with the story of a magician called Robert-Houdin. We came out of the classroom chanting *prez-ti-digi-tateur! prez-ti-digi-tateur!* all along the corridor and into the dining hall.

Then it was Breeze in the afternoon with more mutations and chromosomes and stories of Dolly the sheep.

'Let's hear what part of your origins you're going to explore,' she said.

Dawn W Cheekbones went first. She curled a length of blonde hair around her ear and cleared her throat.

'I have discovered, through extensive research on My Ancestry dot com, Who Are My Relatives dot co dot UK, Heritage dot net, Connections dot org, that I am related, albeit distantly, to the most famous diva of all time.'

We studied her family tree on the white screen. She tried to explain how her great-great-great-great-great-grandfather was Marilyn Monroe's great-great grandfather, which made Marilyn Dawn W's third cousin thrice removed. No one was impressed.

It was my turn. I went to the front. I held up a world map with a red dot over East Africa where humans had begun.

I said, 'Scientists use bits of DNA to find out where people have come from. They've shown that every person on this planet descended from a few thousand people who lived in Africa just a hundred thousand years ago.'

I pointed to the little arrows showing how human beings had spread over the world.

'We could say everyone's history is part of African history because everybody, each and every one of us, came out of Africa.'

'Wonderful, Kofi. Thank you,' said Breeze and her eyes shone brighter than ever. 'Before I was a teacher, I went to Ethiopia on an expedition to the Shungura mountains. I studied bones and stones and genes.

I found skeletons from thousands of years ago. I found out how old the rocks were in which they were buried. And sometimes I was able to take samples from these ancient people to test their DNA.'

I turned to Janie. We stared at each other.

'Expeditions,' she whispered. 'Ancient people.'

'I know, but it can't be her. She can't have done that to Rorty, can she?'

Alice Granger stood up. She put a finger to her lips.

'Sshh,' she said and she spoke in her strange piping voice. 'I think our origins are in the stars. My ancestors rowed down in big boats from the sky.'

There was a burst of laughter but Breeze waved it down.

'Alice has made an interesting observation. Maybe, long, long ago, we did come from other planets, from distant stars. Where did this great ball of rock we call Earth come from? Where did all the elements come from to make it? To make *us*? How far back do we have to go to find out who we are and how we got here?'

'Only The Doctor knows that,' said Hep.

I raised my hand. 'There's something else.'

But the bell rang for the end of school and everyone was on their feet.

Breeze winked. 'Next time,' she said. 'We'll hear about it then.'

Kids poured into the playground and made their way to the gates. I hung around to see if Janie was walking home but she must have already left.

Away from the buses by the fence there was a group of lads, mostly Year 7s. I moved towards them. Saw them muttering. Saw them whispering. I watched their eyes glittering with excitement. More kids arrived. They pushed and shoved and shouted.

A skinny kid called Jon Quix broke out of the throng and came towards me.

'What d'you want?' I said.

'Everyone says you do weird stuff.'

'Maybe,' I said.

'Hocus-pocus and stuff like that.'

'Maybe.'

'They're all scared of you.'

'Good.'

'I'm not.' He stared. 'Go on then. Do something.'

'I might, if you tell me what's going on over there.'

'We're going to Sumo's.'

'Oh yeah?'

'He's going to show us something.'

'What?'

Jon shrugged. 'You have to pay first.'

'How much?'

'A quid.'

I narrowed my eyes. 'You better tell me. I do evil stuff too.'

He shrugged again. 'If I knew what it was I wouldn't be going, would I? Anyway, Sumo says it's something no one's ever seen before.'

I laughed. 'And you believed him?'

Stealth skulked by. He glanced at me then lowered his gaze. Hammer followed. He quickened his step and crossed the road. Jon wandered off and joined the crowd as they drifted down Flores Road.

I followed them but kept my distance. I glanced back to see if Sumo was coming but he must have gone on ahead. Soon they stopped and gathered in his driveway.

I hovered at the end of the road and saw them forming a sort of queue. They were nudging each other, sniggering, shuffling forward. After a few minutes the first ones reappeared, grinning and rubbing their hands. They stopped now and then to show each other how big it was, how long, how wide.

'Worth seeing?' I called out.

A boy turned. 'Yeah. Wicked.'

'What is it?'

The other lad spoke up.

'Can't say nothing. Sworn to secrecy.' He drew a hand across his throat and grimaced. 'Pay a quid and see for yourself.'

'No chance,' I shouted.

It was ages before Jon reappeared. He spotted me and came skipping across the road. 'You going to take a look?'

'No chance,' I said. 'But you're going to tell me what Sumo's up to, aren't you? What's he got in there?'

Jon drew a hand across his throat and made a choking sound.

'More than my life's worth.'

'Don't be stupid, Sumo won't know if you tell me.'

'He said he'd cut our throats and squash us to death, in that order.'

'Don't listen to him. He's all talk, Sumo. He's a big softy really. Bit of a pink marshmallow.'

Jon shook his head. 'I'm not saying anything.' He hitched his bag on his shoulder and headed off.

'Where're you going?'

'To catch the 32M.'

'If I show you some magic will you tell me?'

He stopped. He looked at the ground. Pondered a while.

'OK then. But it better be good.'

I left him in the back garden. I told him to close his eyes and wait. I went in to get Rorty and we came out by the side of the house, out of Jon's sight, and stood in the shade by the garage. Rorty camouflaged himself.

'Jon. Over here.'

He opened his eyes and ran over.

'You got a quid?'

Jon put his hand in his trouser pocket. He brought out a coin. 'It's my bus fare,' he moaned.

'It's all right. This isn't a disappearing trick. Hold the coin flat on your palm. Check it's real. Check it's solid.'

Jon felt it. He pressed it.

'Happy?' I said.

He nodded.

'Squeeze it tight.'

He wrapped his fingers around it.

'*Ata!*' I shouted, and waved my hand over his fist. 'Notice I haven't touched anything. Now open your hand.'

Jon drew in a sharp breath. Two pound coins sat on his palm. He shrieked. He squawked. He jiggled his legs.

'How?' he gasped. 'How did you do that? Do it again. Do it again.'

'Once more, then you tell me everything.' I glared at him.

He nodded, pulled out a fiver this time.

'Fold it three times,' I said. 'Hold it tight.'

I waved my hands over my head, under my arms. I muttered strange incantations. Fluttered my eyelids. Turned three times to the left. Three times to the right.

'*Ata! ATA!*' I boomed.

Jon uncurled his fingers one by one. A second five-pound note, folded in precisely the same way, lay in his palm.

Jon gasped. 'I'm rich,' he said. 'And you're flipping Merlin.'

I brought two glasses of orange juice. We sat on the patio wall by the geraniums. Jon told me how they were led one by one into the garage. How Hammer and Stealth stood on guard at the door.

'Sumo said it was an alien. He told us that the night before there'd been a gigantic green flash and this thing fell out of the sky. But I had a good look at it and I don't think he's right.' He picked up his glass. 'You got a straw?'

I brought him a curly plastic Mickey Mouse.

'And a biscuit?'

I went back for a plate of home-made ginger nuts (visitors only).

'Happy now?' I said.

Jon nodded.

'It's like a monkey, except it's not one. My dad's an expert on . . . what d'you call them? . . . Hominins. I've watched all the wildlife programmes and it's not a chimpanzee or an orangutan or a mountain gorilla.' He counted them off on his fingers. 'And I'm pretty sure it's not a bonobo because they're just like chimps anyway. It's quite small. Lying down on straw. There was a bucket of water next to it. It's like a little monkey-girl.'

A shock ran through me. I held the image in my mind. I stared at him.

'What else?'

'Dunno. It looked ill. It didn't move much. Probably dead, or something.'

He sucked on the straw. He looked up at me. 'You won't tell Sumo, will you?'

'Only if you don't breathe a word about the magic. I do evil stuff too, remember?'

Jon stared at me for a moment then bent down and pulled a mobile from his bag.

'Look,' he said. He tapped a couple of times and turned the screen towards me.

'Took it when Sumo wasn't looking. It's a bit dark but you can see the outline.'

There was something lying on its side. Its eyes were closed.

'What's that?' I pointed. There was a pale object in its hand.

'A daffodil,' said Jon.


I didn't know he'd been standing behind us. I didn't know he'd seen her shadowy figure on Jon's phone.

I found him upstairs. He was painting her in ochre and earthy red. He drew a circle, a pale spidery ring around her.

'I's remembrin,' he said.

His eyes were far away. His voice was soft, so quiet I could hardly hear.

'Teeny snips,' he breathed. 'Bitsy-bobs and wincy-bits. Little head pictures all flashin.'

It was as if he was singing to himself.

'I's remembrin. I's climbin − I's four stepbranches from Great Blue, four stepbranches from headtall as KingWings − I's lookin down at greenness, I's seein Pogsy, thumblong on fern floor, I's hearin Pogsy.

'*Oh forest spirit, oh embrace hisself, oh guide his steppin, return hisself with bountiful sweetness.*

'I's feelin her fearfuls tremblin treeskin.

'I's bitin smoke grass, *wengas* all zzzzin and stabbin. I's grippin, I's reachin, I's pushin smoke grass in *wenga* nest. They's flyin frenzies. I's choppin, choppin, I's tastin sweetness.

'*Yo, Yo, I's headtall as KingWings*
*Yo, Yo, I's breathin Great Blue*
*M-bala, M-bala*
*I's bringin smoke grass*
*I's takin sweetness.*'

He breathed out. He looked up at me with deep, brown, smiling eyes.

'Is Pogsy,' he said. 'Is what I's doin here. I's searchin Pogsy Blue.'

# part two

# 17

'You know when you said there's never only one of something?'

There was silence on the end of the phone.

'You were right,' I said.

Janie gasped. 'You're kidding me.'

'I'm deadly serious. She's in Sumo's garage and we've got to get her out. Tonight.'

It was my idea. Doctor Loopy, Janie called me. Mister Flipping Crackpot, she said. I'd planned it down to the last detail. Janie would be 'doing homework' at mine. I would be 'doing homework' at hers. She would bring her brother's old pushchair with hood and covers and we'd put Rorty in it and walk down to Sumo's. Janie would wait outside and act as a lookout. Rorty and I would slip down the driveway, he'd make a hole in the garage, I'd carry Pogsy from the garage to the pram and we'd leg it back to my house.

Simple.

Practical.

Brilliant piece of planning.

It was about seven-thirty. Going dark. Dogs were yapping. Kids were shrieking in the street. We left Janie on the pavement.

'You're heading for certain death,' she whispered.

'We're doing it for Rorty,' I said.

The garage was a scruffy wooden shack with double doors and a pitch roof. Its tiny windows were boarded up and there was a thick chain around the handles. I gestured to Rorty to slip round the back. He lifted the Hat, drew a hole, clicked and we stepped inside.

A weak light filtered from the kitchen into the dark space. There was a thick scent of animal. We saw our breath in the cold air.

'Are you there, Pogsy?'

We clambered over battered suitcases. Gaping bags of screws and nails. Along another side, shelves were crammed with boxes of mobile phones, DVD players, flat screens, Xboxes. Rorty swiped at the cobwebs. He shifted a stack of fence panels, pulled at bits of netting and plastic sheets.

'Pogsy?'

We balanced on coils of electric cable. I gently pushed jam jars aside with the tip of my shoe. Rorty gasped at a metre-high plastic Santa.

'It's not alive,' I whispered.

We were at the front near the double doors. We could barely see. We crouched and groped about.

'Pogsy? Are you here?'

Rorty knocked a metal bucket.

'Careful,' I said.

We swept the floor with our hands. We pushed our way into corners and up walls into dark, dusty spaces.

I heard him sigh and squeezed his shoulder.

'I think she's gone,' I said.

I caught my foot on something hard and stumbled and fell against the garage door. It eased open and I saw one end of a chain dangling in the moonlight.

'The chain's broken. We can go out this way,' I said, but Rorty wanted to check it all again.

We inched our way towards the back. Poking in all the corners. Opening drawers, little cupboards.

Shuffling through the rubble and the trash and out into the biting air again.

Rorty stared at the ground.

'We're not giving up.' I turned to him. 'We will find her. I promise.'

I tiptoed through the shadows to find Janie, crouching by the wall.

'Oh no! She wasn't there?' she whispered.

I shook my head.

'I'm going in the house,' I said.

'What? How?'

'Rorty's going to camouflage me.'

'No, don't let him. What if it goes wrong?'

'We've got to know if Pogsy's there. It's the only way.'

'This is getting dangerous, Kofi. Rorty's never camouflaged anyone else before.'

'In principle it should work.'

'And what if it doesn't? Are you happy to look like a piece of wall for the rest of your life?'

I drew a deep breath. 'You better go home. I don't know how long it'll take.'

'I hate this,' she said. She stood up and huffed, then gave me a hug. 'Just take care, OK? And let me know when it's all over.' She turned quickly and walked the pushchair back down the road. 'I hate this,' she shouted.

The back door stood open. There was no one in the kitchen so we crept in and found a place where I could hide. Without hesitation, Rorty pointed, drew a huge oval on the wall, clicked to camouflage me, then went outside to wait.

I was crouching in the downstairs hall of Sumo's house, squashed between a folded pushchair and a tower of magazines and newspapers. By the stairs lay a rolled-up nappy and a pile of stained baby clothes. The carpet was thick with dust and flecked with bits.

Nausea rose from my stomach and I tried to swallow it down. I imagined what would happen if I threw up. Anyone walking by at that moment would see a spray of sick coming from nowhere because I was completely camouflaged by Sumo's hall wallpaper.

A woman came thudding down the stairs. She paused to stub out a cigarette on the bannister.

'Get your own grub tonight, ahright? Y'dad and me going out.'

'He's not m'flaming dad,' yelled Sumo. His voice came from the next room.

A baby cried. *Wah-wah-wah-waaaaaaaaa*, like a miniature machine gun. Sumo's mum lit another cigarette and coughed.

'Pick 'er up, can't yah,' she shouted.

She thumped past and smacked open the living-room door. The crying stopped only to start up again.

'Gerr'er bottle,' she said.

Sumo tramped down the hallway. I pressed myself to the wall and held my breath as he came past. I looked down at my wallpaper-shaped body and my carpet-coloured feet. I couldn't believe I was in Sumo's house. I couldn't believe I was invisible.

Sumo was taking the baby's bottle from the microwave when a car door slammed outside. He ditched the bottle on the kitchen table and thundered into the hall. He scooped up his discarded coat, flung it over the stair rail, straightened his trainers on the mat, tucked his bag under the coats and hovered, staring at the front door.

The baby kept on crying.

Sumo went back for the bottle and, after another glance at the door, disappeared into the living room.

Soon after, a man walked in. He was stocky, with broad shoulders and tattoos snaking down his forearms.

He kicked the door closed behind him and went for a pee in the downstairs toilet. He belched and left the room without flushing.

'Col! S'*EastEnders*!' yelled Sumo's mum.

Voices boomed from next door. Screaming. Slamming. Drama at the Queen Vic. I started to edge along the hallway but the living-room door snapped open and Col appeared. I squeezed my feet to the skirting board, closed my eyes. The floor thumped as he walked past. I heard the fridge door, the pop-fizz of a can, a draught of air again then the living-room door banging closed. I breathed out and tiptoed back to the corner of the hall.

A bit later Sumo's mum appeared. She looked in the hall mirror, daubed blue on her eyelids and red on her lips.

'She'll need feeding again, ahright?'

'We're out of milk,' said Sumo.

'Buy some.'

'I need money.'

'You've got y'rown dosh.'

Col appeared. 'You giving your mum a hard time?'

Sumo shook his head.

'You look after my daughter, ahright?' He jabbed Sumo's shoulder. 'Ahright?'

'Ahright,' said Sumo.

They left. The engine started up. Music blared from the open window. Sumo stood at the door and watched them go.

'Hope you die soon, Col,' he whispered.

The baby cried and cried. I squeezed my eyes closed as Sumo lifted the pushchair from my side. He set it down by the front door. He went into the lounge and brought the baby. She was dressed in a furry suit with a hood. Her face was pink. Her eyes were tightly closed. Her arms and legs were stiff with screaming.

'Shh,' he kept saying, 'Shh. Shhh.' He tipped back the seat and laid her down. He tucked the blanket around her. 'Shh-Shh. Shh-Shh.'

He dipped into his school bag and brought out a handful of pound coins, letting them fall into his pocket. He took a bunch of keys from the windowsill, opened the front door, swivelled the pushchair and wheeled it out into the dark.

I stood for a moment in the silence listening to their voice-echoes. I pictured them. Her thin red lips. The meaty fold at the back of Col's head. Sumo's great form cradling the baby.

I looked up the stairs and imagined him there. I followed his footsteps over the threadbare carpet, past the clothes strewn over the bannister and the dirty cups and plates on a tray. Moonlight shone in. My shadow loomed large over his door.

'NO IDIOTS', it said. 'KNOCK OR DEATH'.

His room overlooked the back garden. Weak smudges of orange light glinted through the curtains. A dressing gown clung to a bent rail. Corners were heaped with clothes and mess. There were plastic bags full of stuff. The place reeked of sweat.

Next to Sumo's bed was a cot. A makeshift mobile dangled above it – plastic spoons, reels of coloured cotton, slivers of foil attached with lengths of wool to a pyramid of metal coat-hangers.

He'd sliced 'DEATH' and 'KILL' into the wall above his bed.

I went next door to his mum's room and opened the wardrobe. I lifted the bed covers and peered underneath, pulled out suitcases and heaved them open.

I checked the bathroom and searched amongst the mess in the box room at the front. I thought they might have moved her. I was hoping to discover her asleep in a little space somewhere, a grubby corner, a cardboard box. But there was no place for her here.

I left through the back door. Rorty clicked and my wallpaper disguise disappeared.

I shook my head. 'I'm so sorry, Rorty.'

We headed home. Above the glow of the streetlights the stars twinkled and the moon gleamed. Along the pavement, waste bins stood ready for morning collection. Rorty walked in silence. His head was bowed and his hood was pulled down over his face. We started to cross the road when he stopped suddenly. He turned and set off back towards Sumo's house. He was moving so fast I had to run to keep up with him. We reached the drive and stood a while gazing at the bits of broken wood by the front door and the roof tiles and the junk stacked under the hedge.

'What's wrong?' I whispered. 'What are you doing?'

But he just stood there, rigid and serious.

A dog trotted by. Its claws made scratchy sounds on the tarmac. It paused, sniffed, lifted a leg and moved on.

Rorty didn't seem to notice. He was staring at the garage. I heard him inhale. I watched him raise his right arm, knock the aluminium foil from his head, and point. He guided his finger slowly around the shape of the garage then gave a loud click. An abandoned wheel that had been leaning on the garage wall rolled, wobbled, tipped on its side and came to rest with a clatter on the concrete.

All around it was dark empty space.

The garage had vanished.

# 18

It was still dark when my phone buzzed. It was a text from Hep.

**Weird alert. Sumos garage vanishes without trace.**

I sighed, closed my eyes and lay back on the bed. I imagined the message zipping from one phone to another.

Sumo to Stealth. Stealth to Klenkie. Klenkie to Hep. Hep to me.

I tried to sleep again but couldn't. I kept thinking of Pogsy. She'd been there in the garage after school then three hours later, she'd gone.

And I kept thinking about all the bits and pieces in the garage. Metal, wood, rubber, plastic and all the particles that hold them together.

Molecules. Elements. Atoms.

Leptons. Quarks. Hadrons.

I wondered where they were. All that rubbish and junk, all those trillions of tiny pieces annihilated in nanoseconds. I thought, astonishing things like that just don't happen, and I felt like I was in the middle of something that wasn't real any more. I muttered to myself.

'Please protect the innocent. Please don't let this end in death and destruction.'

I listened to the faint hum of traffic and Rorty's quiet breathing and drifted off again until the alarm sounded and it was time for school.


I walked in through the gate as usual. Up the front steps. Through the entrance. There were clumps of kids, girls in twos and threes, one little nutter hurtling down the corridor.

Hep lumbered up to me. His shirt was hanging out. There was a bit of crusted snot in his nostril.

'Theory,' he breathed. 'Sumo's monkey turns out to be a highly trained undercover reconnaissance unit. The US government send in a crack SWAT team to apprehend said primate and eliminate all evidence. What d'you think?'

'I think you're crackers,' I said.

Everyone kept coming up with a different theory about the garage. Sumo had sat on it. The council had removed it. Aliens had abducted it. It had been destroyed by Spontaneous Garage Combustion. The teachers were just as daft.

Sumo sidled over at breaktime. He nudged me. He gave a stupid grin, waved his hand and shouted,

'*Ata! Ata!*'

'I'd be careful about saying that out loud,' I said.

'You're the flaming magician, not me,' he said.

Hammer and Stealth skulked in the background as if they didn't dare come closer.

'Where did the monkey come from?' I said.

'None of your business,' said Sumo.

'Where is it now?'

'How do I know?'

'You've seen what I can do so you'd better start talking.'

Sumo's eyes shifted.

'Can't talk 'ere,' he said. 'I'll come round to yours.'

'Tonight,' I said.

'Can't,' said Sumo.

'After school tomorrow.'

'I'll see if I can,' he said. 'Start of the holibobs, in't it?'

'You better be there. You don't want your house disappearing as well, do you?'

Sumo shuffled off with his hands in his pockets.

'What was that about?' asked Hep.

'Dunno,' I said. 'Think he's lost it.'

The whole afternoon Janie and me tried not to look like we knew exactly what had happened to Sumo's garage. We wondered about Pogsy Blue. What did Sumo know? Was she wandering around somewhere in Bradborough or had someone taken her?

For the first time ever, Breeze was late for our lesson. She rushed in through the classroom door with her hair all out of place and her skirt on the wrong way. She'd even forgotten her lipstick. She stood at the front and said, 'For the duration of this lesson I do not want to hear anyone mention the word "garage".'

'She's a bit touchy,' whispered Janie.

'Yeah, I wonder why,' I said.

Janie and I met up again after school. We were going to look for bones in Burrows fields, for the Origins project.

She was wearing a waterproof jacket and her Lake District walking shoes.

'How did he make the garage disappear?' she said. 'I mean, what did it *actually* look like?'

I tried to conjure up the image and replay it in my head.

'It was dark. He was upset about Pogsy not being there. He just did his pointing thing and clicked. The garage was there. Then it wasn't.'

'No fizzling out or anything?'

'Like deleting Sumo's face paint,' I said. 'There one second, gone the next.'

She sighed. 'Have you thought what you could do if you could make things disappear?'

'I'd start with evil teachers, then violent parents and move swiftly on to psychopaths.'

'I'd get rid of nuclear waste, rubbish tips and greenhouse gases,' said Janie. 'And no more wars. Think of that. I mean you'd have hardly started a fight before it was all over.'

'Delete the enemy before they've drawn their weapons.'

The thought of it was terrifying.

We followed a cycle path behind the houses.

'This way,' said Janie. We turned into a narrow road then on to a footpath. 'D'you think that Gerry guy knows what Rorty can do? D'you think he knows about him copying and camouflaging and painting?'

'I'm not sure. He knows about the chip because they were tracking the signal from it. And maybe he knows Rorty can camouflage and that's why they used the Hound from Hell to pick up his scent.'

'Or maybe,' said Janie, 'they only go searching at night because they don't want to be seen, so they wouldn't be able to see Rorty in the dark, camouflaged or not, and that's why they needed the dog.'

'Possible,' I said, but I didn't really believe it.

'Imagine if someone really evil got hold of him.' Janie suddenly sounded afraid.

I shuddered. Thoughts like that had already flooded my mind. I'd had visions of someone forcing Rorty to delete the Houses of Parliament and the White House. I'd thought of him copying nuclear weapons, cloning the President, mass-producing bank notes.

'He's so gentle,' I said. 'He comes from a misty forest with tiny antelope and exotic birds. I can't bear the thought of someone using him for something terrible.'

'Well, we'll not tell anyone,' said Janie. 'Let's swear we'll never tell, not even under pain of death. Let's swear to protect him. With our lives.'

We stopped on the path. She rested her hands on my shoulders.

'I swear to protect Rorty with my life,' we said. 'Even under pain of death.'

'And that includes finding him somewhere to hide,' added Janie.

'Working on it,' I said.

'It also includes finding Pogsy Blue,' said Janie. 'D'you think they're boyfriend and girlfriend?'

'I think that's a definite possibility.'


We walked on through woodland to Burrows fields. We climbed a wooden stile and looked at the deep furrows and the rows of little green shoots stretching to the sun.

'This is where Mum's family's from,' said Janie. 'They were farmers, going back generations.'

It had rained overnight, exposing rocks and stones. The earth was littered with them. Janie bent to pick up something. She gazed at it then chucked it back at the soil.

'University bods have been excavating up here. They've found loads of pottery. Zillions of pieces.

Dates back to 700 BC, some of it. But what I'm really looking for is a bone. I'm not being greedy. Just one little bone, then they can test the DNA and see if I'm related.'

We searched the ground, squatted on ridges and crumbled clumps of earth with our fingers. We listened to the croaking calls of the rooks and felt the breeze in our hair and smelt the rich tang of the soil.

'I'm starving.' I flopped on to the grass.

'Look in the rucksack,' said Janie. 'I'm going to try nearer the survey site.'

She'd brought blueberry muffins. There was half a loaf and a knife and a nearly empty carton of margarine. She'd stuffed a bag of salt and vinegar in a side pocket. There was a plastic Noddy cup and a steaming flask of sugary tea.

I made a crisp sandwich. I gazed at the line of trees along the field and glimpsed the fuzz of new green on their branches. I watched Janie in the distance, picking away at the ground, searching for her ancestors. And I wondered what we were going to do about Rorty Thrutch.

Janie trudged back and slumped by my side. She'd found a bone but it looked too small to be human.

'I'll keep it anyway,' she said. 'You never know.'

The air cooled and the light began to fade. We packed up and headed for home.

'Been thinking.' I sped up to walk alongside her. 'About what Jon said when he showed me Pogsy's photo. He said his dad's an expert.'

'On what?'

'Hominins.' I glanced at her. 'Gorillas. Chimpanzees. Orangutans. Humans.'

'Is Rorty a hominin?'

'Almost definitely,' I said.

'D'you think Jon's dad has something to do with it then?'

'That's precisely what we have to find out.'

# 19

It was two days since Rorty deleted the garage. The sky was angry and grey. Rain had started pelting down again. I heard the doorbell. Sumo was standing on the mat. The chain was on and I was looking at him through the gap.

He'd brought the baby. She was fast asleep in a pink sling strapped to his chest. He peered around me into the house.

'Mam in?'

'No.'

'Dad?'

I wondered why he was asking. I wondered if he knew that I'd hidden in his house, been in his room, and now he was going to get his revenge. But he wouldn't try anything, would he? Not with the baby.

'Dad should be back any minute,' I said. It wasn't true but I glanced down the drive as if I was expecting him.

The baby started to cry. Sumo pulled a bottle from his coat pocket.

'She's hungry,' he said. 'Need to warm the milk.'

I undid the chain. He wiped his shoes, slipped them off and straightened them on the mat. We went to the kitchen. He heated the milk and shook little drops on his wrist. He eased the baby out of the sling, sat down and pushed the teat into her mouth.

'Her name's Shima,' he said. 'Mam's idea. It's an island in Indonesia. She's on lates tonight at Tesco's.'

I looked at the baby. Her eyes were scrunched up closed. She was making little gulping sounds.

'Police have been round 'bout the garage,' he said.

My heart fluttered and bumped. I thought of all the chatter at school. All the theories and stories. *How's that ruddy great wooden structure been plucked from Number 113 Mendel Crescent without a trace?*

'Col thinks I did it. He's mi stepdad. But we know it were you, don't we? And you know how to do magic. And I want you to teach me.'

I hesitated. I shook my head. 'I don't really do magic, Sumo. It's an illusion. Magic doesn't exist.'

'You told me you'd done it.'

'That was to get you to come round here so you'd tell me about the monkey.'

'Don't believe you. You're pure magician, mate. Who d'you geddit from? Y'dad?'

I shook my head again. 'I'm telling you, the paint stuff was a trick, that's all.'

'Nah, nah, nah. The paint wasn't no trick and the garage wasn't neither. It disappeared in ten minutes. I went out. It was there. I came back. It was gone. No noise. No vans. No mess. Who else could o' done it? Any case, Stealth saw you hanging round after school when we took the kids to see it.'

Sumo eased the teat from Shima's mouth. He lifted her, laid her over his shoulder, rubbed her back. He studied me through his small hooded eyes.

'If I tell you stuff will you get rid o' Col?'

I stared. I didn't know what to say.

'Put a curse on him, you know, make him disappear?'

'I told you. Magic doesn't exist. Anyway, it'd be criminal. Murder even.'

Sumo grinned. He shook his head.

'You're a rubbish liar. I was covered in green paint, you waved your arms, blahdyblah-blah, the paint was

125

gone. You knew we wouldn't let you in the garage, so you got mad, and hocus-pocus, whizz-bang-blotto. Don't take no genius to work that out.'

He gazed at Shima. He drew the baby in. Kissed her. Touched her button nose. He stood up and tucked her against his huge frame.

'It's not me I'm asking for,' he said.

He hadn't eaten so I made him beans on toast. Two tins. Six slices. He showed me how to hold the baby. He told me to be careful and pointed out the parts of her skull that hadn't yet joined. She gazed up at me. She gurgled. I touched her tiny fingers and even tinier nails. I smelt her soft milky smell.

Sumo scoffed down his food. Licked his lips. He used more bread to mop up the juice.

'I won't hurt anyone,' I told him. 'And I don't do magic.'

He looked at me. He nodded and grinned.

'But I want you to tell me what they were looking at in the garage. It's really important. If you help me, I promise, somehow, I'll help you out with Col.'

Shima cooed and gurgled in my arms. Sumo wiped his mouth on the back of his sleeve and sniffed. He straightened the knife and fork on his plate. He folded his arms on the table.

'Two weeks ago, Col was coming back from Jimmiz, 'bout two or three in the morning, and he sees this monkey-thing on the roundabout by the uni, just lying there it was, so he stops the car, gets out, looks at it, bit exotic you know, not your usual gorilla-urangitangi-type thing. He thought he could make him some cash out of it so he brought it home and kept it in the garage. Thought he could sell it to a circus in Eastern Europe or something. He's been drugging it to keep it quiet. I've seen him crushing Mam's pills.'

Sumo glanced at his empty plate. 'Got any more grub?'

I passed Shima back to him. I offered him Bio banana bread. He took two slices.

'What sort of monkey was it?'

'It's like nothing you've ever seen. It's like Planet of the flipping Apes. I was making a bomb out of it. Twenny-five quid in one hour. I could have sold it myself but now you've messed it up, haven't you? Coz it's gone now, hasn't it? Along with the garage and all o' Col's stuff.'

Thunder growled. A strong gust blasted rain bullets at the window. I fixed my eyes on the table. I didn't dare look at him.

'Does Col know Quix?' I said.

'Jon Quix?'

'His dad.'

Sumo sniffed. 'Knows loads o' blokes. Probably. I dunno. Why y'asking?'

'I think, what actually happened was . . . someone took the monkey before the garage disappeared. I think it might have been Quix or someone called Gerry working for him. Only she's not a monkey. She's more evolved than that. And we absolutely have to find her. It's a matter of life and death. And I need your help.'

I dared a glance. He was grinning again. He was shaking his head. Shaking with laughter.

'I help you. You help me. Whizz-bang-blotto. I knew it were you. You're a magician you are. Flipping magic man.'

# 20

'You did what?' squeaked Janie. She pressed her hands to her face. Her eyes burned at me through her fingers. 'What are you? Sovereign Emperor of the Lost Marbles?'

We were in the bookshop café. Level two. Leather chairs by the window. Me: herbal tea with dandelion, elderflower and Himalayan goji berries. Janie: hot chocolate grande, caramel, maxi-froth and double marshmallows.

'I had to tell him, Janie. Sumo's the only link we have to Pogsy.'

'*Had* to Pogsy. We've no idea where she is now.'

'Pogsy was at Sumo's house because his stepdad took her there. It's the last place she was seen so it's the logical place to look for clues to find her. Col will be looking for her too and Sumo will tell us if he finds anything.'

'What did Col want with Pogsy?'

'Thought he could make money out of her. Circus, or zoo, or something.'

'Are you sure she was taken from Sumo's house? She didn't just walk off by herself?'

'I told you. Someone broke into the garage. The chains were cut.'

'Maybe she cut them. Maybe she's like Rorty, you know: copy, cut, delete, paint. Maybe Pogsy woke up from her tranquillisers and cut her way out. Yeah, that would make sense. She must have a chip in her head, like Rorty.'

'I don't think so.'

'Why not?'

'Because if Pogsy has a chip, Rorty would have been able to contact her long ago. Remember how he sent me messages? He would have been able to do the same to Pogsy, chip to chip.'

'Not if she was drugged the whole time, except at the end. Sumo told you they ran out of pills.'

'Then why hasn't she contacted Rorty since she escaped? It's two days since she disappeared.'

Janie huffed and folded her arms. 'You're *so* annoying.'

I shrugged. 'Natural brilliance. Anyway, it could be Gerry who took her. Sirus could have sniffed her out, so Gerry and his mob will still be looking for Rorty and now they know Col's involved maybe Gerry'll go back to force more information out of him.'

'Hadn't thought of that,' said Janie. 'Does Sumo know about Rorty?'

I shook my head. 'I didn't want to complicate things. Best he doesn't know for now in case he's forced to tell Col.'

'By the way, I googled *Professor* Quix,' said Janie.

'Me too, but there's not much about him, is there? He goes on expeditions. Writes publications about Neanderthals and that's about it.'

'But he has the brains to be the evil mastermind.'

'Certainly does,' I said.

'So let's go and interrogate him. Now!'

'Do you think he's going to admit that he's illegally experimenting on two hominins? There must be another way of finding out what Quix is doing. Like I said, Sumo will be watching Col and he'll tell us if he hears anything.'

Janie's eyes narrowed. 'So your worst enemy is now your bestest buddy? What did you bribe him with?'

I drew in a deep breath.

'OK. This is where it gets tricky. I promised to help him out with Col and before you ask, I don't know what that means exactly but Sumo thinks I'm a black belt, fifth dan in the Dark Arts and can probably wipe Col off the face of the planet.'

'With Rorty's help he's probably right.'

'So I'm his friend now.'

'Lovely,' said Janie. She bent over her mug and blew a smiley face in the froth.

We watched the shoppers scurrying along Corn Market Street. Skinny boys in droopy jeans. A black woman with pink-streaked hair. A man in a fluorescent jacket picking up the litter.

My phone buzzed.

'Rorty,' I said.

**Needin bits an bobs is ravishin**

I looked up at Janie. 'I think he means ravenous.'

'Who's ravenous?'

'The Molimo.'


We set off for Tesco's to buy bananas, lettuce and a packet of custard creams.

'What on earth is a Molimo?' asked Janie.

'It could be another way of finding Pogsy. It's a bamboo pole. A sort of totem and a ceremony and a musical instrument all rolled into one. The Forest is like a god to Rorty. It gives shelter and warmth and food and when things go wrong, like losing Pogsy, he thinks it's because the Forest, *his* Forest, has been asleep.'

Janie stared at me sidelong. 'A bamboo pole? That eats custard creams?'

'It's symbolic. Feeding the Molimo is like giving offerings and when he plays the Molimo it's like saying a prayer and it wakes up the Forest and the Forest is happy again.'

'And Pogsy Blue reappears?'

I nodded. 'Something like that. Once he's woken the Forest he's going to play the Molimo on roundabouts and that'll bring Pogsy to us.'

'Weird,' said Janie.

'I know.'

'I like weird.'

'I know that too. The first ceremony is at midnight tonight.'

'Bit late for me,' said Janie, looking disappointed.

'Don't worry,' I said. 'I'll tell you all about it tomorrow.'

# 21

There's a patch of ground in the corner of our garden behind the shed. You can't see it from the house. It's shaded and a bit narrow and according to Dad, 'a devil to get the mower down'. Mum calls it 'the Meadow', which is a bit of a stretch since it's not much bigger than a bathtub. I'd pretty much forgotten about it until Rorty asked for a quiet, sacred place for the Molimo. He laid it down gently amongst the clover and stinging nettles.

A couple of nights ago, he'd been to Beads Botanic Gardens. He'd slipped down the thick stem of the Virginia creeper outside my window into the moonless dark. Cave-black, he called it. He'd disguised himself as a piece of night sky, then made a hole in the brick wall of the garden centre and crept in amongst the palms and orchids and bonsai trees. He'd dipped his fingers in plastic pools, smelt the hyacinths, heard the guinea pigs scuffling and the fish tanks blooping. Then he'd pulled a piece of bamboo from a basket, copied it, replaced it, made his way out again and closed up the hole.

It was midnight. We stood in The Meadow looking down at the metre-long pole nestling in the grass.

'What happens now?' I said.

Rorty turned to me. 'Is Bad Dead.'

We took the bananas, lettuce and custard creams and laid them on the ground next to the pole. He sprinkled water over it and wrapped it in a tartan blanket from the back of the car.

Then we sat there with it under the stars. Venus hovered low in the west. Pinpoints of light flickered above the bright planet.

'That's where we're from,' I said, looking up. 'Every part of us, each tiny little piece was forged in stars like those. When a star dies, it creates all the bits that make our skin and blood and hair and nails and the leaves and trees and animals of the forest. Of your Forest, Rorty. Everything. Every single atom on this earth.'

Rorty gazed upward. He sighed.

'And our planet is just a giant ball hanging in the blackness, like the stars and all the other planets. Surrounded by darkness and nothingness.'

Rorty pointed and drew a shape in the sky. He pointed at himself and clicked and became a dark twinkling mass. He danced about. He lifted the Molimo to the night sky to show it where it had come from. He rubbed it with soil and grass and leaves so that it understood that it was part of the earth in which the Forest grew. We took it to Burrows brook just over the fields. I followed his sparkling shape through the gloom.

'Look at you, Rorty!' I said. 'You're a starman!'

He smiled and laid the Molimo in the water and told it that without water the Forest would be Dead and Gone For Ever. Then we returned to the Meadow. Rorty clicked, reappeared and raised the Molimo to the heavens once more.

'Forest is father an mother,' he said softly. 'Forest is givin bountifuls. Is givin eatins an coverins an cozies an cuddlins.'

He paused. He breathed.

'Wen Forest is sleepin is wen is not watchin and carein us.'

I imagined Rorty's misty Forest giving him everything he needed. Food from animals and plants. Water from rain and rivers. Wood and leaves for huts and fires. A forest to worship and to protect him.

Rorty clicked. 'Wen Forest is sleepin we's needin wakin Forest. We's needin Molimo singin. An wen we's singin we's wakin Forest an Forest is carein us agen. Forest is findin Pogsy Blue.'

He settled himself on the ground. He put the Molimo to his lips, drew in a long breath and blew. It made a sad, haunting sound like he was calling to Forest with all his heart. I imagined the notes dancing on the breeze, tumbling through leaves and branches, and the Forest waking and the gentle sounds winding their way round streets and towns and villages, slipping under each door and into every window, until they found Pogsy Blue.

When he'd finished, he laid the Molimo amongst the clover and stinging nettles where its shape melted into the dark. And for the first time I saw a tear in Rorty's eye.

We crept into the house, our shadows shifting with us up the stairs. We buried ourselves in the soft warmth of our beds and listened to the night creatures.

'Quix,' I whispered. 'Do you know that name?'

I held my breath. I blinked in the darkness.

'Quix,' Rorty whispered. 'Quixie. Is makin Rorty fearfuls. Is makin shudderins.'

I stretched out my arm and found his hand.

'What do you remember?' I breathed.

'Is fringy. Is wispy dreams an shadow-glooms in far-far starry night. Is flutterins an whisperins in deep, deep caves.'

'But you remember the name?'

'In bitsy-bobs. Tincy-snips an snaps.'

'Tell me, won't you, if you remember any more? It could help us find Pogsy. Let's sleep now. You're safe here. You're safe here with me.'

## 22

I don't like parties. I hate pointless chitter-chatter. I don't care if the Super Hoops are up for relegation. I don't want to know if Carly got off with Wilso so I usually end up in a corner on someone's PlayStation. And if you're not much fun, word gets round and you don't get invited any more. Which is perfectly fine by me.

But in the first week of the holidays I invited myself to a party. It was Sumo who told me about it. He'd been invited because he liked sausage rolls, crisps and cake, but I think it was more because Jon Quix didn't dare say no. I was there because I wanted to know if Quix was hiding Pogsy.

It was on Saturday at three o'clock. Jon was going to be twelve.

*

Little Crompton-on-Leigh was half an hour by bike. It was five past three when I pulled up outside the iron gates of the Manor House. Balloons and bunting hung from stone pillars. There were cars parked on grass verges. There were beeps and shouts as drivers tried to turn in the narrow lane. Kids leapt out with presents and cards. Some wandered in with their mums and dads.

'It's round the back,' they were calling.

I pushed my bike along the driveway. There were lines of purple crocuses and yellow primroses. Sprinkles of bluebells under the dome of a sycamore.

The gardens were huge. There was a bouncy castle between two marquees. Chairs and tables had been set out on the patio. I left my bike leaning on a wall.

It was all boys. They were wild already. Charging and screaming and throwing each other about. Jon spotted me and the smile fell from his face. He hesitated, then plodded over.

'Merlin,' he said. 'What are you doing here?'

'Just thought I'd come along,' I said.

'Has my dad been talking to you?'

'No,' I said.

'Phew! That's good then.' Jon looked relieved.

'Think I'll keep Sumo company for a bit. Is that all right?'

Jon shrugged. 'S'pose so. There'll be thirty-three of us altogether. It's going to be awesome!'

There were screams. The boys on the bouncy castle were building a human pyramid to launch someone over the top. 'Jon! Jon!' they called.

Jon roared and charged off to join them.

I spotted Sumo sidling around the food tables, helping himself to an iced bun and a slice of cake.

'Lovely nosh,' said Sumo. 'You having some?'

'Not yet.' I scanned the gardens. 'Which one is Jon's dad?'

Sumo shrugged and the iced bun disappeared in one mouthful.

'That day at your house,' I said, 'when the kids came to see the monkey, after the garage disappeared, did anyone else come round?'

He chewed and thought.

'Yeah,' he said. 'Later on. After Mum and Col got back from the pub. Heard 'em outside shouting. Made a real racket. Woke Shima up.'

'Who was it?'

'Dunno.'

'What did they want?'

'Dunno. Someone's always after Col for something.'

He snatched up a couple of sausages on sticks.

'By the way, she's called Pogsy,' I said.

'Nice,' said Sumo.

'Ready to go inside?'

'Yeah, course,' he said.

'Don't spend too long. Remember she's not going to be wandering about, so we're looking for small spaces and locked doors.'

We went in through the double doors on the patio. We heard chattering and chinking teacups in the kitchen. Jon had stuck up signs – 'TOILET THIS WAY' – but we took no notice of them.

'I'll go upstairs, you look down here,' I whispered. 'See if there's a basement. Meet you on the patio in ten minutes.'

Sumo headed down a corridor and I charged up the curved staircase. I worked my way down the landing counting six bedrooms and three bathrooms. I powered round each one, checking in wardrobes, under beds, looking for locked cupboards and places where a small hominin could be hidden away.

At the end of the landing was another, narrower

staircase. It led to an attic room. I knocked and slowly pushed open the door.

'Anyone here?' I said.

The room was huge, with windows along the length of the sloping roof. There were tables for snooker and table tennis, a model railway snaking around the walls. At one end, across the width of the room, was a line of cupboards. I heard a faint tapping from somewhere.

'Pogsy, I'm Kofi, I'm Rorty's friend. Call if you can hear me. We've come to take you home.' I stood still and closed my eyes trying to hear a little knock or her voice. 'Pogsy, are you in here?'

I crept closer, pulled on a door and peeped in. There were shelves packed with board games and children's toys. I shifted them about to make sure I could see right to the back. I stretched to feel if there was a false door. The tapping started again. It was hard to hear where it was coming from.

'Pogsy? Don't be afraid. I'm here to help you.'

I tried another cupboard, slowly pulling the door open, and another, each time hoping I'd see a pair of bright little eyes staring out from the dark.

The last cupboard was deeper, full of books and more toys. I climbed inside. I called softly.

'Rorty is safe with me. Come out and I'll take you to him.'

My elbow knocked a stack of hardback books which toppled on my back, spilling a storage box full of Lego over the floor. I froze, hoping no one downstairs had heard, and in that moment there was a clatter of wings on the roof. Immediately the tapping stopped.

Birds pecking on the roof, that's all it was. *So where are you, Pogsy Blue?*

I closed the door and made my way downstairs. I was almost on the ground floor when I saw Gerry at the bottom leaning on the bannister. His forehead was a row of tight furrows.

'You again,' he said. 'Keep popping up in all the wrong places, don't ya? What y'doing in here, kid?'

'Toilet,' I said. 'The sign was pointing this way.'

'Sure you wasn't snooping?'

I held his gaze. 'What would I be snooping for?'

Gerry scowled. 'You wait to see what the Prof has to say. He's looking for you. He wants to have words.'

That didn't sound good. What did Quix want with me? Unless Jon had told him about the magic.

Sumo was waiting outside. 'No basement,' he said. 'Couldn't find nothing downstairs.'

144

'I didn't find anything either.'

'We'll find 'er, mate, don't worry. Hungry work that. Let's do a recce on them tents. Looks like there's more grub down there.'

'Yeah, looks like a good place to hide from Quix for a bit as well.'

One of the marquees was empty apart from a table and a few chairs. The other was done out in purples and blues with giant painted flowers lining the pathway. Inside hung huge paper lanterns above tables packed with more flowers and marshmallows and tiered cake stands. I imagined what Rorty would have done if he'd been here – copying all the cakes and jellies so he could eat birthday food any day he liked. It was a good job he was safe at home and didn't know anything about the party.

'Hullo there,' said a voice.

A white-haired man with a deeply tanned face and dazzling blue eyes came over. He smiled. 'Professor Nigel Quix. Jon's father. Call me Nigel.'

I took in a sharp breath.

He shook our hands. Patted our shoulders. Studied us each in turn.

'I'm Kofi,' I said.

'Sebastien,' said Sumo. 'Nice place y'got.'

Nigel beamed. 'Yes, we rather like it. I've heard of your father, Kofi. He works at the university, doesn't he? Very interesting line of research.'

'You won't know my dad,' said Sumo. 'I don't even know my dad.'

There was a slight shift in Quix's expression. 'Oh. That's a shame,' he said.

'What's your line of research, Professor Quix?' I could hardly believe how calm I sounded.

'Oh, this and that. *That*, mostly.' He laughed. He swept back his fringe. 'We were going to have a magic show today but we've been let down at the last minute. I don't suppose either of you could give it a go?'

Nigel's blue eyes peered deep into me like he was dissecting my thoughts, peeling away my little secrets.

'Kofi's brill,' said Sumo, 'he does all that flashy stuff, y'know, magic paint an all that, yeah.'

'I think you've mixed me up with someone else, Sumo.' I glared at him, trying to make him stop.

'Nah, you do proper magic. The real deal. Don't need no props. A few magic words, bit o' hocus-pocus and whizz-bang-blotto.'

'Shut up, Sumo.'

Nigel laughed. 'So we have a volunteer?'

'Sorry,' I said. 'Sumo's mistake. I really *can't* do magic tricks.'

Nigel moved closer. He stooped to whisper. 'That's not what Jon tells me.'

I felt hot suddenly. My heart stuttered and thumped.

'Told ya,' said Sumo. 'You was just being modest. You're that good you could probably be on telly.'

'I have every confidence in you, Kofi,' said Nigel. 'The boys will love it.'

'This is ridiculous. I've never done a magic show.'

'Come on, Merlin,' said Nigel. There was an edge to his voice now, a sternness. He gave me a firm push and steered me round the bouncy castle. 'Let's get out there and see some of your little party tricks, shall we?'

# 23

Jon's mum was herding the boys into the empty marquee. They sat huddled on the grass, whispering and giggling and making rude noises with cupped hands and damp armpits.

One of the other mums was laying things out on a trestle table. Coloured handkerchiefs. A pack of playing cards. Foam balls and metal cups. A black and white plastic wand.

'Might come in useful,' she whispered. 'Just let me know if you need anything else.'

Parents trickled in carrying wooden chairs. It was starting to look like a crowd. A real audience. I tried to make myself breathe deeply and slowly but my heart was clattering. I saw Jon. His face was flushed. There were damp strands of hair stuck to his forehead.

'He's *really* good,' he was saying. 'Just watch.'

'Um. Welcome,' I said, above the chatter.

The boys clapped and whooped.

'Um. I haven't prepared anything in particular . . . er, so let's start with a card trick.'

I picked up the pack. I shook the cards from the box. Some of them scattered on the floor and I stooped to scoop them up. A few titters rose from the front.

'Can I have a volunteer?'

A boy on the second row thrust his hand in the air.

'Go on, Marty. Go on!' His friends pushed him forward.

Marty joined me. He straightened his T-shirt, folded his arms across his chest and grinned back at his friends.

I shuffled the pack. Fanned out the cards, face down. I turned away.

'Pick a card,' I said. 'Look at it. Remember it. Show it to everyone. But no one shout it out.'

I opened up the deck and Marty returned the card. I shuffled again.

'Now, by the powers of magic, I will find your card.'

I dealt them on to Marty's open hands. I picked one.

'This is your card!' I said.

'No it isn't,' said Marty. He held it up for everyone.

They shook their heads. 'No it isn't,' they said.

There was a chorus of sympathetic groans from the mums.

'Have another go, pet,' said one.

'Do the money one!' shouted Jon.

'We want the money one!' said his friends.

I put the cards back on the table. 'I will now perform the balls and cups trick.'

A wave of grumbling and muttering passed round the tent. I set three balls and three cups on a small table. I had no idea how the trick worked. No idea what I was going to do.

A little girl approached from the side. She held out the plastic wand.

'Forgot this,' she said.

'Aw!' sighed the mums.

'Three balls. Three cups,' I said. I placed a ball under each cup.

'By the powers of . . .'

'Not again,' said Sumo.

'OK then.' I waved the black and white stick dramatically over the cups. 'Hocus-pocus, whizz, bang, BLOTTO.'

I lifted one cup. There was empty space beneath.

There were gasps, then silence.

I tipped the second cup. Again, the ball had gone. A cry came from the boys.

I lifted the third empty cup triumphantly into the air.

'Whizz-bang-blotto!' shouted Sumo. The boys got to their feet cheering and clapping. The mums joined in. The little girl trotted over and tried out the wand.

I turned my back to the crowd and fingered the handkerchiefs and the playing cards.

'Rorty, what are you *doing* here?' I whispered. 'You've got to leave before Quix finds you.'

'I's helpin findin Pogsy,' he whispered.

'One more card trick and that's it. Then put the Hat back on and go.'

The noise was getting louder. The kids were chanting, 'We want more! We want more!' I wasn't sure if Rorty had heard me.

The dads had been chatting outside and came in to see what all the fuss was about. I saw Nigel with them. His face was red and veins were bulging on his neck. He was giving instructions to Gerry.

My heart banged in my chest.

'So for the final card trick today . . .' I said.

'But you've only just started!' shouted a boy at the back.

'Sshh,' said the mums.

I shuffled the cards again then noticed some of the little kids wriggling down from their parents' laps. I glanced over and saw great swathes of blue appearing on the side of the marquee. The children were transfixed. Their gazes followed the band of colour sweeping and swirling over the tent.

'On the other hand,' I said, 'maybe we'll do magic painting. Well, we have blue.'

I pointed and smiled. My hands swept in circles, right to left, left to right, chasing the emerging colours.

'And some gorgeous yellow.'

The audience were suddenly on their feet. Jumping up and down. Whistling. Shouting. Everyone's eyes were on the tent.

I tried to make it look as if I was doing it but it was impossible to anticipate where the colours were going to appear.

'And black,' I said. I tried to follow the outline of two emerging eyes and a pair of large boots. Three kids squeezed under the tent to the other side. One wriggled back. He looked disappointed.

'Nothing there,' he shrugged.

'Looks like a blob,' I shouted, attempting to draw them back from the other side. 'Well, blow me, it's a nose!'

The little ones jumped up and down. They screamed. They clapped.

'Clown. It's a clown! See that! It's a clown!'

There was a swarm of little bodies slapping the nose and shoes and smiling face. Jon and his friends approached, hands stuffed in their pockets. They examined the mural, stood back, scratched their chins.

'Awesome.'

'Genius.'

'How did he do it?'

I watched the parents, saw the disbelief on their faces. I listened to the rumbling of their voices. They knew it wasn't possible. One of the mums stood up. Her face was beaming.

'Hasn't he done well? Absolutely bloomin' marvellous! Don't you think?' She held her hands above her head and clapped. 'Come on, everyone.'

Others stood and smiled and applauded. I tried to smile back but all I wanted was for Rorty to be on his way home.

'How did you do-oo that?' said Nigel Quix slithering between chairs and around bodies. 'Quite astonishing.'

He patted my shoulder. 'I suppose it comes off?' he said.

'Sorry?'

'The paint? They're collecting the marquees tomorrow.'

He stared at me for a second then laughed. 'Just kidding, just kidding.'

Something distracted him. He looked beyond me to the garden. He raised his eyes and nodded. I turned and saw three men with three dogs.

'You know what, Kofi?' he said. 'We've missed out on the birthday cake. Let's have some in the garden.' He waved to a couple of boys, bent down to speak to them and watched them race off towards the house.

He put a firm hand on my back and steered me behind the marquees to the rose beds and tall willows. We sat on a wooden seat on a grass ridge, looked out over fields and hedges, as far as the eye could see.

'It must be marvellous to have a talent like yours,' Quix said. 'Did you see those boys? They loved it. Absolutely loved it.'

I was hunched over. Pressing my palms together. Staring down at the grass. I shrugged. 'It's nothing really.'

'And do you apply yourself to everything with such vigour and perfection?'

I shrugged again. 'Pretty much,' I said.

Quix leaned forward so he could see my face.

'I'm very glad you came here today. Do you know why?' He said it softly, like he didn't want to frighten me.

I glanced at him. Tried to pretend I didn't know.

'You've formed quite a bond with the creature, haven't you?'

I felt heavy suddenly, like I was tipping and couldn't stop. I sat up and breathed, trying to shift the heaviness away.

'It's been missing for some weeks now. I'm glad that it's survived. Have you been helping it, Kofi?'

He was gazing at me, speaking gently, choosing his words carefully.

Three boys came tearing across the garden, carrying plates. 'Here's your cake.' They gave us forks and napkins. They waited, laughing a bit and nudging each other.

'Go on, ask him.'

'You ask him.'

'Can't.'

'Go on.'

'Jon says you do a trick with money.'

I shrugged. 'It's really not that impressive.'

'Jon says it is. Can you do it? Here I have a quid.' He held it out to me. 'Please.'

Nigel spoke. 'If it's all right with you gentlemen, Kofi and I are having a little business chat. He'll be joining you in a while. OK?'

'Is he going professional?'

Quix laughed. 'Always a possibility, don't you think?'

They nodded and started to walk off. One turned.

'What's the dogs for, Mister Quix?'

'Oh, just security.'

'Think they've found something. They're letting them off their leads.'

Quix got to his feet and shaded his eyes. 'Must have caught its scent,' he muttered.

*Rorty!* I stood up too. The trees and sky blurred. The sun burned down on me.

I put the plate on the bench and watched the boys running down to the hedge and the fields beyond. The dogs were barking now. I wanted to leave. I just wanted to rescue him, get on my bike and go home.

'Shouldn't take long,' said Quix. He was watching intently like it was a horrible kind of sport. 'The thing is, it has acquired skills I had not anticipated. Quite astonishing skills.'

There was yelping now. The sound of men shouting. Kids at the hedge were jumping and screaming. Quix strode over the lawns, weaving his way through the flower beds, but I was sprinting, tearing across the garden, shouting for Rorty.

I reached the edge, where there was a little gate into the fields. I looked up into the trees, hoping Rorty was hiding there.

Then Quix arrived. He pushed his way through and strode over to Gerry and the others. He yelled. He waved. He told them to call off the dogs.

'What's going on?' said Sumo.

'Dunno,' I breathed.

Quix waded through the tall grass. He spoke to the men. We saw them shrugging and shaking their heads. We saw Quix slap his forehead, throw his arms in the air.

There was no sign of the dogs. Not a sound. Not even a whimper.

*He's deleted them*, I thought, *Rorty's gone and deleted four dogs.*

I turned to Sumo. 'Really think we should go now,' I said.

Sumo sighed. 'Yeah, me too. Couldn't eat another thing.'

# 24

It took us two hours to get back. It was my fault. I kept looking behind to see if Quix and Gerry were coming after us. I was checking on Rorty too, who was following quietly and trying to blend into the background.

We took the back roads and hidden lanes and footpaths through fields, which was completely pointless because they knew exactly where I lived.

Still, it gave me time to think. And as I was wheeling my bike, I thought: *So now we know. Professor Nigel Quix. Wimpy Jon Quix's dad. The same Jon Quix who cried when they ran out of chips on second lunch service. Different sort of chips now, isn't it?*

*So Nigel is the mysterious someone who brought Rorty here from an undiscovered corner of our planet and put my dad's invention in his head. The incredible smarty-pants who made the silicon chip work in ways my dad had never dreamt of.*

*Or maybe not.*

*Quix said Rorty had acquired skills he hadn't anticipated. So MINDLINK must do amazing things but only in Rorty's brain. So, clever old Rorty. Outsmarting Mister Smarty-Pants himself. But if Quix still wants him back, what's he planning to use Rorty for?*

*And what a cheek calling him a* creature. *Prehistoric genius, more like.*

We took turns on the bike. We drifted down hills, tried short cuts, lost our way. Sumo kept blabbing about how we should go into business. Become partners. Said I'd be on TV in no time.

'You haven't forgotten about Col, have ya?' he said.

'All in good time, Sumo. All in good time.'

Janie dashed over as soon as we got back.

'Did you find Pogsy? Was she there?'

I shook my head. 'Sorry.'

Janie buried her head in her hands and growled with frustration.

I told her about Quix and Sumo and the deleted dogs.

'So it's true, Jon's dad's behind it. And Gerry and the mob are working for him. Evil creep.'

'He said Rorty's been missing for weeks. So I guess once you discovered you could delete things, like making a hole in a wall, you escaped from Quix? Is that what happened, Rorty?'

'Did Pogsy escape too?' said Janie.

Rorty thought for a moment. 'I's no head pictures. I's not remembrin.' He looked sad suddenly and scrambled on to Janie's knee. He ruffled her hair and picked out little flakes of dry skin.

'I only washed it yesterday,' said Janie. 'You're going to make it worse.'

But Rorty was concentrating. He didn't seem to hear.

'You shouldn't have come to the party,' I said to Rorty. 'It's made everything a whole lot more tricky.'

'I's likin parties,' said Rorty, 'I's likin cake.'

'We have to get you away from here before they come looking for you again.'

'I's good at deletin,' said Rorty.

'Deleting dangerous dogs is on the limit of acceptable but you must never delete people. That would land us in real trouble. We need to get you to somewhere safe. Out of reach.'

'On that subject . . .' said Janie.

'What?' I said.

'I've found somewhere.'

'Really?'

'Yes, really. It's got everything. It's in the middle of nowhere. Dog-proof. Masses of firewood. Fresh water. Loads of fish and space to build a waterproof hut.'

'Where?' I said.

'That's classified information.'

'Come on, Janie.'

'You wouldn't know even if I told you.'

'Everything on the list?'

'Everything.'

'Is new house?' said Rorty.

'Yes.' Janie took Rorty's hand. 'Just for you. We'll take you there next Sunday. But tonight, you two are going out with the Molimo. I wish I could be there but it's too late. Mum wouldn't let me.'

'You won't have to wait long, Janie. Rorty'll play the Molimo when we go to the new place, you'll see.'

# 25

He woke me with a gentle whisper. We crept out of the quiet house. We slipped along the streets like we were trespassers, intruders in the still, silent night. The moon was rising and the stars were sparkling down on us. We tottered along the central white lines. We pressed the buttons at crossings and ran to see how far we'd get before the lights changed to red. There was barely a noise. A dog yapping. The whine of a motorbike. The soft purr of cars on the dual carriageway.

Rorty looked up.

We stepped on to the Tesc-O.

Another circle. Everything works in circles. The sun, the moon, the earth. Spring, summer, autumn, winter. Clouds, rain, sea, clouds. Planets around suns. Electrons around nuclei. Rorty's hut. Rorty's fires. Traffic around a ring road. Car wheels on a roundabout. Rorty's breath through the Molimo.

He stroked it. He whispered to it. He shuffled and flexed his arms like a soloist before a concerto. He drew a vague shape over the moonlit sky, made a click and sat down in a pool of stars.

And the Molimo began to sing.

I imagined his Forest. I pictured him alone under the shimmering towers of green with the Great Blue above. I could almost hear the buzz of insect wings and the squawks and trills of birds and smell the earthy stench of soil and mud. And there was Rorty with the great God of the Forest and the goodness and the beauty of the world all around.

The soft sounds of the Molimo drifted over Bradborough.

*Find her*, they sang. *Find Pogsy. Bring her home to us. Bring her home.*

I opened my eyes and the night was still shimmering and the moon was still gleaming and the song of the Molimo stayed with me as we walked home under the orange streetlights. It was there when I put on my pyjamas and flopped into bed. In my wakefulness and in my dreams I heard it calling.

*Stay awake, stay awake, we are lookin, we are seekin, we are searchin Pogsy Blue.*

## 26

It was the last Saturday of the holidays. The day before Rorty's moving day, and even though he wasn't moving far we thought it would be nice to buy him a leaving present.

We left him in my room and went downstairs for lunch. Mum had prepared a white and green bean salad, two Pink Lady apples (cored and cut in half, covered in lemon juice to prevent browning), mixed nuts and raisins (no salt, oil or additives), carrot juice, and a single prune. There was a note:

Potassium-rich lunch. Put prunes on shopping list.

I looked at the food. 'I can't survive on this.'

'Don't moan. It's good for you,' said Janie. 'It's what early man used to eat.'

'If early man had the chance, he'd be scoffing fish and chips and a Magnum for afters.'

166

We cleared up and set off to The Fat Fryer to get Rorty's surprise.

Or rather, we didn't.

At least, not from The Fat Fryer.


Mum once told me that if you're destined to be somewhere in the space-time continuum, everything becomes effortless.

'Listen to this, Kofi,' she'd said. 'Last Friday, I knew I was meant to be at Beads Botanics at 3:45 p.m. because when I arrived in the totally full car park in the burning sunshine – for which I was forced to switch on the air conditioning for the first time in two years – a car was just backing out of the only space that was shaded by the verdant boughs of an oak.'

'*Verdant boughs*? That's a bit poetic for you.'

'Don't be cheeky,' she said. 'That afternoon, something happened at the surgery that has never happened before. I had a whole hour with no appointments. I took one glance at the flowerless orchid on my desk and without another thought off I went to the garden centre. I arrived back in the surgery, calm, cool . . .'

'You're never calm and cool,' I said.

'I was that day,' said Mum, 'totally Zen I was, carrying a fully endowed Dendrobium, just as my next patient walked through the door.'

She keeps a list of the times when she's slipped into the space-time vortex where everything merges effortlessly as if it were written down somewhere in *The Great Book of Planning*.

I didn't want to admit it, but she had a point.


Janie and I didn't know that we were meant to be in the Valley Road chemist's at 1:10 p.m., but everything came together to make sure that we were.

We'd set off to buy Rorty's fish and chips from The Fat Fryer, which is in completely the opposite direction to Valley Road, but on the way we met Hep, who told us that The Fat Fryer was closed due to a fire caused by a build-up of grease in the ductwork. He suggested we try the Salt 'N' Battered.

On Valley Road.

I had exactly the right change in my pocket for one cod and a large chips and we were coming out of the shop when Janie noticed the chemist's next door.

'I'm going to get some anti-dandruff shampoo,' she

said. She checked her purse. 'It's four twenty. I've only got four.'

I searched my pockets and shrugged.

'Never mind then,' she said and we turned to leave.

Leaving at this precise time point was not ordained in *The Great Book of Planning* and this is why the space-time vortex gave Janie a gentle nudge, enough to make her glance down at the pavement where she saw a twenty-pence coin.

'Just what I need,' she said. 'That's amazing.'

At 1:09 p.m. we entered the Valley Road chemist's. There were three aisles. Shampoos happened to be in the central one opposite baby products. At 1:10 p.m. we bumped into Breeze, who was carrying a basket containing one Bumper Pack of nappies and three packets of baby-fresh wipes.

She seemed embarrassed.

'Oh hello,' she said. 'Have you enjoyed the holidays?'

'Yes, thank you,' said Janie.

'Those fish and chips smell good,' said Breeze, possibly meaning that we should be getting on with eating them and not paying so much attention to the contents of her basket.

'They're for a friend,' said Janie. She smiled. Then she asked the question that we had no business asking, that both of us were desperate to know the answer to, and only Janie had the cheek to ask.

'Someone had a baby recently?'

Breeze paused. She gave a loud 'Hmm'.

'Yes. They're for a friend,' she said, going over to the counter to pay.

Janie bought the anti-dandruff shampoo and we watched Breeze leave the shop.

She waved. 'See you both on Monday.'

We headed home to get some more money, then back to Mr Barty's to buy a white Magnum.

'Can't possibly be hers,' I said. 'There'd have been a bump.'

'Some women don't have big bumps, and she always wears those loose flowing tops and dresses.'

'If it was hers she'd be on maternity leave,' I said.

'That's true,' said Janie. 'Then who are the nappies for?'

Breeze hadn't been in Bradborough long. All we knew was that she used to travel the world excavating fossils and had joined Landlow four months ago. She'd said that she was gradually getting to know her neighbours, who were all ancient and crumbling, and apart from that, she hadn't made many friends.

None of us knew then that we were supposed to see Breeze in the Valley Road chemist's that day, but Mum was right, some things need to happen. It was ordained. It had been written down on a page somewhere in *The Great Book of Planning.*

Back home, Rorty opened the greaseproof package with the tips of his fingers. He smiled at the whale-size cod and thick-cut chips. He copied them, together with the white Magnum.

'Don't eat them every day though,' said Janie, 'or you'll get fat.'

Rorty had been copying food for a while – apples, bananas, chicken stew – ready to move to his new home. From Janie's description it had everything he could wish for. And he'd finally be safe from Gerry, Sirus and Professor Nigel Quix. We hoped.

# 27

The river was deep in places. It flowed silently over pebbles and stones. Little gusts ruffled its surface. It gleamed like a strip of bronze.

We were heading for the far bank where the trees shadowed the water. We pushed the yellow dinghy over the edge. We heard it scraping rocks, saw the ripples it made in the shallows. I held it steady as we climbed in. There was only room for two. It would be me and Rorty first, then me and Janie.

We crouched on the soft corrugated floor. Janie balanced the Molimo across the bow and Rorty grabbed it with one hand and let the other hand trail in the water.

We headed upstream and caught the flow midway. It carried us swiftly. I tried to push across to the pebbled shore but we were stuck in little eddies and swirling water. Janie shouted from the bank to pull harder but the paddles were small and the current was strong. Rorty kept leaning over the sides to look at the fish.

'Is biggies,' he said. 'Is teeny-tiny tiddlies and big-bigger-biggies.'

He rocked the boat. He bumped it up and down. He threw his head back and laughed as we spun hopelessly downstream.

'Stop messing about!' Janie screamed.

'I's lookin at fishies,' said Rorty.

'Better do what she says,' I whispered. 'She's dangerous when she's stroppy.'

We reached the end of the island then turned back and approached along the far bank where the river was deep and calm. It was cool under the outstretched branches. Rorty grabbed the overhanging leaves and moved us towards the shore.

It was called Heron's Island. Janie's dad used to fish here until the river became choked with floating pennywort. It was everywhere. Vast green mats clinging to the water's edge. Rorty stepped on to the pebbles carrying the bamboo pole above his head.

'Have a look round,' I said. 'I'll get Janie.'

*

There were nettles up to our waists, thorny stems as thick as fingers. We found sticks and slashed at tangled briars. We trampled down thistles and snapped stems that oozed milky sap. Odd musty smells seeped through the earth – foreign scents of onions and sweet herbs. We paused to breathe and wipe our faces.

'Come see. Come see.'

Rorty was swinging his legs from a branch. He dropped down in front of us.

'Is loveliness. Is all shinies and sparklins.' He pulled us through patches of cow parsley and thistles.

He'd made a clearing at the end of the island where the bank fell steeply to the river. He'd chopped patches of dense undergrowth and lopped off the tops of trees leaving freshly sliced stumps poking through the earth. Around the clearing the uncut grasses leaned outwards as if a huge draught had blown them down. It was like wading into a deep grassy bowl.

I pulled Rorty's new Hat from the rucksack. It was an upgraded 3000 SS Turbo featuring a foam-backed brow pad to prevent forehead indentations and ventilation slits to improve airflow.

'I designed the flaps,' said Janie. She helped Rorty fit

the Hat to his head. 'Flaps-Up means MINDLINK works perfectly. Flaps-Down and nothing works, no send or receive or anything. Flaps-Down and you're just your everyday hominin.'

Rorty beamed. 'I's tryin,' he said.

Rorty lifted the flaps that were positioned above the scar. He went over to a sycamore and wrote 'HOMININS RULE!' on the trunk.

Janie laughed and clapped.

Rorty closed the flaps and tried to delete the writing but nothing happened.

'Yeah! It works,' said Janie. 'You have to remember to keep the flaps down most of the time so Gerry and Quix can't find you.'

Rorty nodded and beamed. He lifted the flaps once more and deleted the writing on the tree. Then his expression changed and he pointed to a space at the end of the clearing.

'Kofi. Janie. Is sittin.'

We sat down and watched him gather scraps of lichen and sticks and logs. He squatted beside us. We saw the concentration on his face and heard the click from the back of his throat. A stick with a notch and a stick stripped bare appeared in his hands. It was the fire-drill, the one he had made by the hut all those weeks ago.

Janie gasped. 'I'll never get used to that,' she whispered.

He set the stick in the notch and rubbed back and forth until smoke streamed and the lichen burst into flames. He fed the fire with twigs and dry grasses and he sang, so, so softly, as if he was singing to the fire itself.

'*Hey-yo balaya-yo*

*Hey-yo balaya-yo*.'

He was singing to the fire and he was singing to the Forest.

'Forest needin wakin,' he whispered.

The smoke was a thin spiralling plume. Rorty stood before us, solemn and calm.

'I's listenin,' he whispered. He tipped his head to one side and closed his eyes. 'Forest is breathin. Forest is sleepin. Is darkness evry places. Darkness in Forest an darkness in chuldrins an darkness in brothers an sisters. Wen Forest is sleepin we's need wakin Forest. We's needin singin. We's needin hearins, voices of oldens, spirits voices, we's need wakin Forest an Forest speakin us agen.'

176

He edged around the fire, stepping carefully. He looked at us and said, 'Is time. Is Molimo,' and he turned and walked into the trees.

# 28

A wind had got up. Clouds belted along like the sky had been switched to fast forward. Janie pulled her jumper round her shoulders and shuffled closer to the fire.

I wasn't sure if it was the Molimo at first. We heard short blasts and groans. Then it came, unmistakably, from deep in the wood. A long gentle moan full of sadness and yearning. An ancient sound that felt its way through the earth and through the air into our blood and into our bones.

'Did you hear that?' said Janie. 'You can sort of feel it inside.'

I knew it, but I didn't say. We closed our eyes and listened.

'Which forest is he waking?' said Janie. 'Maybe it's the forest here, near where Pogsy went missing. Maybe the Molimo is calling to the forest spirits, the oldens, the spirits of people who lived here long ago.'

'I suppose so,' I said. 'If you believe that sort of thing.'

Janie hunched her shoulders. 'Sometimes you have to be a bit mystical and mysterious. Let go of your facts and let your imagination fly. Let go of your molecules and your sound waves and your electromagnetic thingummy-jigs and use your instincts and your feelings. There are things we *don't* understand, you know. Tell me how a flipping garage disappears using current scientific knowledge?'

I didn't try. What could I say? No one knew. No one could explain it.

We sat quietly, just listening. The trees swayed and shuddered to the rhythm of its voice. I found myself moving too as if it was somehow alive, not just a voice but a presence, a being, whispering to us, feeling its way into us and around us. I stood up. I shook my legs. Shook my arms. Walked about.

Janie smiled. 'It's getting to you, isn't it?' she said.

'No. No. I'm fine.'

The Molimo paused then started up again. It was further away now. It filled the trees with its haunting voice. Above the island, nimbus-grey clouds gathered and thunder sounded. Large droplets began to fall.

'Waterproof hut!' said Janie, suddenly. 'He's completely forgotten the hut!'

The rain came down in waves as if the air had a pair of lungs, just a smattering on the in-breath then a deluge that battered us towards the shelter of the trees. In moments Rorty was beside us peering out at the storm.

'Hut,' said Janie, wiping the drips from her eyes. 'What are we going to do about the hut?'

Rorty took a step forward. He swiped his hand through the air and a sudden draught blasted down that forced our eyes closed and made us gasp. A large wooden structure had landed inside the clearing, followed by a tremendous clatter as gravity brought its contents to a sudden halt.

'Now that's really *not* possible,' I said.

We dashed for the doors, unravelled the cut chains and squeezed inside.

'No one move,' I shouted, 'there's loose nails and paint pots and an inflatable Santa.'

'How do you know?' said Janie. 'I can't see a thing.'

It wasn't completely dark. Slivers of light slanted down through the ill-fitting doors. We squatted until the hammering rain subsided and we could open the doors and see the tangled mess inside.

'How did you bring it back?' I said.

'I's wantin little house for Pogsy. I's thinkin teeny-tiny thinkins far far aways. I's doin accidentals first times. I's whooshin grasses all down-down. Now I's knowin where I's findin teeny-tiny thinkins. I's bringin Pogsy little hut.'

Janie laughed. She shook her head. 'You mean Sumo's garage has been sitting around somewhere waiting to be brought back?'

'Sort of makes sense,' I said.

'Does it?' said Janie. 'Does it really?'

*No,* I thought. *No it doesn't. It makes absolutely no sense at all.*

Rorty moved through the rubble, gradually clearing it into small heaps. I stacked the stolen computers and TV screens in a corner. We flipped a small chest of drawers on its side as a makeshift table and Rorty produced three cod and chips and a Magnum for afters.

The sun slanted low over the trees, lighting only the topmost branches and leaving the rest in deep shadow. Clouds slid into delicate layers of pinks and bluey-greys.

'What d'you think then?' said Janie.

'About what?' I said.

She raised her eyes skyward. She whispered.

'You felt it, didn't you? The expectation, like something important and mystical is going to happen.'

I shrugged. 'Not really.'

She tutted. 'Blooming hopeless, that's what you are. Flipping block of granite. I didn't imagine it you know. I'm not making it up.'

I couldn't say anything. I knew it couldn't be true, but the echoes were still there, in my head and in my limbs. Like a slow pulse, like a heartbeat. Like the Forest was slowly waking.

**29**

'Merlin! Merlin!'

It was the first morning back at school. I was at the top of the steps. His legs were a blur. He raced towards me clinging to the straps of his backpack.

'Wait!' he said.

I turned and waited.

Jon tore up the staircase. There was terror in his eyes.

'Dad made me tell,' he said. 'I know it's my fault but he made me tell him everything.'

I stared longer than I needed to. Long enough to make him fear me, to feel the power I had over him.

'That day you did those magic tricks in your garden, Mum wanted to know why I'd caught the late bus and I said I can't say and Dad said you owe your mother an explanation and he shouted and I said I'd been watching magic tricks and Dad asked what magic tricks and I said really cool stuff and I showed him the five-pound notes and he looked at them and he went all serious and made me tell him about the monkey.'

He breathed hard and deep.

'And now you're going to do evil stuff, aren't you?'

'Probably,' I said.

Later, in the assembly hall, Mr Steele was announcing the school's fundraising activities for World Hunger Day when Jon Quix lurched into the centre aisle and threw up. Students recoiled around him like soap on floating pepper. He was led away by Tiggy-Winkle, our school nurse, and after a shortened assembly we all trooped out past the caretaker who was scooping up the rest of Jon's breakfast.

'It's my fault,' I said.

'Why?' said Janie.

'I scared him this morning. He looked like death.'

'What did you do?'

'I let him think I was going to put spells on him.'

'Then you better tell him the truth,' said Janie.

*

We found him at lunchtime. He was alone, leaning on a wall. His face was milky white.

'You all right?'

He twisted away as I approached.

'I need to tell you something,' I said.

Jon stayed motionless, staring at the ground.

'I'm not Merlin. I can't do magic, or black magic, or any sort of magic. Sorry.'

Jon shrugged and sighed. 'If that's true, how did you make a five-pound note from nothing and how did that clown appear and how did the dogs disappear?'

'Come and sit down,' said Janie. She steered Jon to the steps in front of the dining hall. She handed him some lemonade and he took great gulps from the bottle. We sat next to each other waiting for someone to speak.

'It's my dad, isn't it?' said Jon.

'We think so.'

'I thought he was doing research. What's he really doing?'

'We were hoping you'd tell us that.'

'Is it criminal?'

'Not sure.'

'What's an archaic hominin?' He stared at us with wide, searching eyes.

'Our closely related extinct ancestors,' I said.

Jon blinked. 'I think my dad might have one in his lab. But that was quite a long time ago.'

I looked at Janie.

'So what are we waiting for?' she said. 'I'll just wander in and say, *Hi, Prof Quix, got any illegal hominins that need rescuing from your evil laboratory?* Then I'll wander around looking for Pogsy and wander out again.'

'That's not going to happen, Janie. Obviously. Jon, have you ever been in your dad's lab?'

'About a year ago. I had to show my passport.'

Janie laughed.

'It's worse now,' said Jon. 'Even before you reach Reception, there's key codes and swipe cards, and at night they switch on motion detectors, intruder alarms and CCTV.'

'So the only possible way would be for Rorty to go in,' said Janie. 'Can motion detectors detect something invisible?'

'Who's Rorty?' asked Jon.

The sun had moved and the stone steps of the dining hall felt cold and damp.

'Let's go for a walk,' I said.

We followed the edge of the tarmac where it merged into the playing fields. Jon was between Janie and me, hands deep in his pockets and eyes fixed on the ground.

'We think he's a throwback,' I said, 'a sort of ancient human species that has survived in a remote place on the earth for thousands of years. We think the hominin in your dad's lab is his friend, Pogsy Blue.'

Jon's eyes widened. 'Thousands of years?'

I nodded.

'My dad travels a lot,' said Jon. 'He goes on trips to Africa and Siberia and Indonesia. It's him, isn't it? He's done all this.'

Janie nodded. 'We also think that your dad has something to do with bringing Rorty and Pogsy here to do some sort of experiments.'

'Experiments that wouldn't work on monkeys,' I added, 'but are too dangerous to try on humans.'

'That's not right, is it?' said Jon. He stopped and looked up at us.

'No,' I said. 'That's why we're trying to help them.'

Jon sighed. 'I've heard him talking to people on the phone. He's getting loads of money. That's how he set up the lab.'

We approached the front of the school again. It was almost time for lessons.

'*I* can get in the lab,' said Jon. 'I'll ask him. I'll pester him till he lets me.'

'No,' I said. 'Your dad would know it was something to do with me. You'd just get into more trouble.'

'But I want to help.'

'Even if you got in the lab and found Pogsy, how would you get her out?'

'Kofi's right,' said Janie, 'don't involve your dad. Just tell us where the toilets are. I know exactly how to get in. And out.'

Janie's plan involved Rorty, Sumo and a motorbike – she wouldn't say any more – but we needed Sumo's buy-in.

It was at that point that we realised we hadn't seen him all morning.

# 30

He wasn't in school on Tuesday either.

Or Wednesday.

Or Thursday.

In fact he'd been absent all week. Breeze wouldn't tell us why, only that his mum had phoned in to say he had flu. I didn't believe a word of it. So on Friday I made a beeline for Mendel Crescent.

It was late afternoon. Shadows were growing long on the pavements. The privet hedges shone in a golden light. I followed alleyways behind houses, short cuts along the cycle path. I came to a green space, a grassy hillock criss-crossed with sandy tracks. From the top I could see the whole of Crowlands – dull grey rooftops, telephone wires, curls of smoke from brick chimneys. Kids were hurtling over mud ramps on bikes and skateboards. Scrawny, squinty-eyed dogs were prowling the hedges.

It was easy to spot Sumo's. It was the house with the garage-sized gap next to it. I trained my eyes on the back bedroom window.

'What y'goggling at?'

It was a thin girl with stringy hair and tired eyes.

'Seeing if Sumo's in.'

'Fitzy? He's with Shima.' She pointed. 'Up and over and down the other side.'

I turned to leave.

'Did you hear about the garage?' she yelled.

'What about it?'

'Got sucked up in an alien spaceship.'

'Did it really?'

'Yeah. Pity they didn't take that Col with them.' And she strode off towards the swings.

His right forearm was in plaster. The skin around his left eye was black and swollen. His lip had been split and patched up again. He was on a park bench gazing at the pushchair, singing.

'Mind if I sit down?'

He shrugged. He didn't even turn to look at me.

'Col?' I said.

He shrugged again.

We sat a while not saying anything. He hummed and rocked the pushchair.

Shima woke up crying. Sumo sighed and stood up and pulled back the covers.

'Y'having a right mardy today, aren't ya? Them pesky toothies, intit?'

He grimaced and sucked in through his teeth as he tried to lift her without using his bad arm.

'Can I help?' I said.

'Go on then,' he grumbled.

I lifted her and pulled her close. I felt her tiny body. Sumo rubbed pink gel on her gums. He gave her a pink teething ring.

'That should settle her for a bit.'

'We were wondering where you'd got to.'

He tutted and tossed his head.

'Didn't Hammer come round?'

'Nope.'

'Stealth?'

'Sent me a text. "Where are you? On your holibobs?" Daft beggar.'

'Why don't you report Col to the police?'

'Can't prove nothing. He'll say it wasn't him.'

'Why did he hit you?'

'Why d'you think? *All my stuff's missing*, he says. *My flaming livelihood*, he calls it. All the stuff he's nicked, more like. Ten thousand quid's worth of stolen stuff he was gonna sell. Including that flaming monkey.'

'But it wasn't your fault.'

'Try telling him that.'

He tickled Shima's chin. He smiled and pulled funny faces. He stuck out his tongue. Her eyes tried to focus then she stiffened and started to grizzle again.

'Give her here,' said Sumo. 'It's sleepy-time anyway.'

I helped him put her down and tuck her in. He released the brake on the pushchair and we set off down the path.

'We're still looking for Pogsy,' I said. 'Has Col said anything?'

'No. What's so important about it anyway? What did y'call it, more *involved*?'

'*Evolved*,' I said. 'And there's . . .'

I stopped myself. Should I tell him about Rorty as well? I could hear his voice in my head, *You're joking me, right? Two monkeys in the middle of Bradborough?*

'It means it's more human. More human than a monkey. It's like early man, before *Homo* . . . before human beings, like us, lived on the earth. And . . . there are two of them.'

Sumo scowled. '*Two* extinct monkey-humans? What are they doing in flaming Bradborough?'

I laughed. Out loud.

'That's what I'd like to know.'


We called in at Tesco's. I waited outside with Shima. Sumo came through the self-service checkout with a bag of nappies, baby wipes, powdered milk and a bike lock.

'For my bedroom door.'

'What should I tell them at school?' I said.

He shrugged.

'When shall I say you're coming back?'

'Monday. Swelling should have gone by then. Unless he has another go at me.'

I looked at him. Bloodshot eyes, bloodied nose, bloated lip and Shima, a tiny scrunched-up ball of innocent humanness.

'Can you get hold of a motorbike for tomorrow?' I said.

'Yeah,' said Sumo. 'No probs.'

# 31

Operation 'Insomniac Sheep' was to take place on Saturday in broad daylight. It was Janie's idea. No night-time security to worry about and less chance of finding anyone in the lab on a weekend. To be truthful, we didn't have a clue what to expect.

Jon told us that the toilets were round the back so we approached from that direction along a footpath behind a bank of trees. We spotted them straightaway – two elongated rectangular windows for each of the cubicles, a couple of metres from the ground.

Making a hole in the side of a building takes about nine seconds. One second for Flaps-Up, five to draw an oval large enough to pass through, two to think delete, and one to make a clicking sound and for the molecules of the building to disappear. In an instant we were looking at the dividing wall between the toilets. We crept through the hole into a cubicle. I knelt down and looked under the partition.

'All clear,' I whispered.

Rorty closed up the hole in the outside wall and we edged towards the door. I eased it open. We heard murmurings. Keyboards clattering. We peered at each other. Stretched our eyes in surprise.

'So many people,' whispered Janie. 'What are they all doing here on a weekend?'

We could see right through to the reception. Everything was tip-top. Pristine white. There were people in lab coats. There were chrome lights and tiled floors.

We inched into the corridor and pressed ourselves against the white wall. Rorty camouflaged us in turn. It was the first time for Janie. She squeaked in surprise.

'Stay close,' I said. 'Me first, then Rorty, then Janie.'

'How are we going to follow when we can't see you?'

'Hold hands,' I whispered.

We sidestepped along the passageway. We passed a Speech Laboratory with posters of brains and neural maps. There were banks of buzzing computers. We had to shuffle beneath a huge placard called 'Brain Atlas'.

'Did you remember Flaps-Down, Rorty?' I breathed.

He was wearing the upgraded 3000 SS (second generation). One strip of heavy-duty aluminium in place of the multiple foil layers, with paperclip hinges on the flaps to make it last longer.

Rorty tapped my hand in reply.

We shifted a little further to another open door. A team of people was watching a simulation on a huge screen. It showed soldiers on a military operation moving around a war zone in total silence. The only way they were communicating was by sending thoughts to each other. Using MINDLINK.

*So that's what Quix is doing.*

We were squatting behind a water cooler when an office door burst open. Professor Quix strode out. Walrus Gerry and the detector man were behind him. I squeezed Rorty's hand and we froze.

'Our clients want this programme completed,' shouted Quix. His face was flushed, the veins in his neck bulging. 'We haven't even tested the EEG signals in different languages. Operation Silent Talk needs *two* hominins. I don't care how you do it.'

The detector man spoke up. 'We told you we were picking up a signal from one of them. The device was working but it was like the creature suddenly cloaked itself – the signal just disappeared.'

Quix opened his mouth to say something then closed it again.

'Basically they's tricky, Nige,' said Gerry. 'You gotta admit it.'

Quix's eyes fixed on Gerry. He spoke slowly through taut lips. '*I* don't have to admit anything. If the detector doesn't work, *Tom*, it is your job to fix it. In the meantime, use more dogs. *Two* hominins are what I need and *two* hominins I shall have.' He turned and pounded down the hallway.

We waited until all was quiet again.

'You OK, Janie?'

'No,' she whispered. She touched my hand. She was trembling.

I led the way under surveillance cameras studding the ceiling, creeping further into the heart of the building. We kept pressing ourselves to the wall as people buzzed past. We pushed open a door into a windowless room. There were circular lights angled over an operating table. There were white drawers on wheels. Trays covered with blue cloth and shiny silver instruments laid out in a row.

Rorty's white form edged round the space. We heard him sighing.

We moved swiftly to another corner of the building, another room with no view. We looked through the glass panel in the door. There were white bars this time from ceiling to floor, a door in a cage, an open drain, scraps of food in plastic boxes.

'Is this where they kept you?' Janie whispered. 'With Pogsy?' She reached for Rorty's hand. 'I hate Quix,' she breathed. 'I hate all of them.'

I caught sight of a clock. We'd taken twelve minutes already.

'Come on,' I said. 'The longer we spend in here the more chance we have of being caught. We've got to check one more line of offices and the room in the back corner.'

We scurried along listening to the chatter, trying to hear any mention of Pogsy. We made a dash past an open door. I knew it was risky. A woman with designer glasses caught sight of us. She shot out of her chair.

'Hey! Hey! What was that?'

Other workers crowded the corridor. The woman pointed out our shapes. We were hurtling towards room 1.1D. We could hear voices from the other side.

'Deep breath,' I whispered.

Janie tugged my hand.

'We've got to go in. We've no choice,' I said.

I clicked the handle. We crept in on our hands and knees over the white tiles and froze against the wall. We heard Quix's irritated voice.

'Either come in or close the flaming door.'

The lab was cluttered with wires and cables. There were dozens of screens. Tom, the detector man, was working by the window. Quix was near us leaning over a table. There was something half-covered with a white sheet.

'Nigel!' The woman burst in. 'There were shapes. White human shapes. Three of them. They came in here.'

Quix scanned the room. 'It's the other hominin. For God's sake, someone get hold of it!'

He swerved around tables, got on his knees and swiped the floor.

'Camilla, search from that end. The rest of you, block the door.'

Tom scrabbled under benches at the far end. Camilla kicked her pointed shoes into open spaces. She edged towards us, frisking the wall.

We crouched, holding on to each other. There was no chance of escape now. I closed my eyes.

Rorty must have flicked open the flaps because two things happened at once. The detector on Tom's table let out a sharp blast of beeps and Camilla froze in a bended position, which made her glasses slip and her cheeks sag and redden. But before Rorty could disable Quix, he'd bounded over, swiped the space, grabbed Janie and dragged Rorty from between us.

'Finally,' he said. 'Remove the camouflage. All of you.'

32

Minutes later I was pacing Quix's office. Janie was fuming. Tom was tying the upgraded 3000 SS tightly to Rorty's head and another man was binding his wrists behind his back.

'Leave him alone!' I yelled. 'They're the biggest discovery of the millennium. The fact they exist at all is a miracle. They change the entire map of human evolution and all you can do is exploit them. You're horrendous!'

Quix nodded to a thickset man waiting outside the door. 'Lab Three,' he said.

There was nothing we could do. We watched as he shoved Rorty down the corridor.

'One hundred per cent evil, that's what you are,' shouted Janie.

Quix simpered. 'In all of your bravado and brilliance, what you've failed to realise is the technologies we are developing here are vital to the security of our world. They're essential to the future of this planet.'

I held his gaze. His blue eyes burned into mine. 'What *you've* failed to realise is you've kidnapped two unique and harmless beings and you've stolen MINDLINK from my dad.'

Quix's brow crumpled into tight folds. 'There's some clever work in that device. It would have taken us years to do what your father has done.' He paused. 'And, by the way, there are two.'

'Two what?'

'Two chips. Two MINDLINKs. In one brain.'

I glanced at Janie.

'Where did you find Rorty?' she said.

Quix laughed. 'Oh, that's its name, is it? Well, I couldn't possibly reveal that.'

'But it was you, wasn't it? On one of your archaeology trips?'

Quix smiled. 'We have a world map at home littered with red pins. Each time I return from one corner of the world or another, my darling son Jon adds a pin to keep a record of where I've been. I heard the legends of Ebu

Gogo, folk tales of little people, half-human, half-ape, but I didn't think I'd find them alive today, living and thriving in the forest.'

'You could have kept quiet about it,' she said. 'You could have left them alone.'

'How could I?' said Quix. 'They're precisely what we needed. They were, quite literally, our missing link, if you'll pardon the pun. I insist you bring the other one back. We're trying to keep the situation low-key. Handle it without force. But if necessary . . .'

So it wasn't Pogsy on the table. It probably wasn't a body at all. But if she wasn't in Quix's lab, where was she?

'No,' I said. 'No. We will do absolutely everything in our power to keep her away from you.'

I stood up. 'Come on, Janie. We're going to find Rorty, then we're leaving.'

'Are you now?' said Quix. 'Lab One,' he said to Tom. 'No refreshments.'

I side-glanced Janie.

'Plan B,' she mouthed.

I nodded, slipped my phone from my pocket and typed to Sumo:

**Activate Plan B**

Tom pushed us down the corridor. Some of the workers glanced at us and turned away. They shook their heads and grinned like we were a couple of silly kids playing games. We crossed the reception, past sofas and coffee tables and neat fans of magazines.

'Kofi. Look,' said Janie, nodding towards the entrance doors.

'That was fast,' I said.

Sumo was outside holding Jon in a headlock. Plan B was already in action.

The receptionist grabbed the phone and seconds later Quix stormed past us. He strode up to the first set of glass doors and glared. He punched in a code, stepped through and froze. Sumo banged on the glass with his plastered arm. He shook his head. He drew a hand across his throat. Quix pressed the intercom and Sumo's calm voice came through.

'Let them out or Jon disappears. There's a motorbike waiting. He'll be gone and you'll not see him again.'

Jon grimaced and struggled. He seemed tiny next to Sumo.

Quix took a step forward. Then back again.

'Hurry, Dad! He's choking me to death!'

Sumo started to back away, dragging Jon over the tarmac.

Quix slapped his head. He puffed and blowed.

'Just call the police,' Quix said to the receptionist.

'You won't see Jon again if you do,' I said.

Quix shouted to Sumo through the intercom. 'OK. OK. Come back. For God's sake, just give me time to think.'

Sumo moved in closer again. He stared at us through the door. His face was still swollen and bruised. 'Bring them two where I can see 'em,' he said.

'Do as he says,' said Quix.

Tom pushed Janie and me forward.

'Get rid o' them thugs!' yelled Sumo.

Quix gestured for other security men to move away.

'Thing is, Prof Quix,' said Sumo, 'I know what you're up to with Col. You've been round our place a few times, haven't ya? You and 'im are cooking little plans, aren't ya? Now, what if them little plans were to leak out?'

'There are no plans,' said Quix. 'Let Jon go.'

'Oh, still breathin', is he?'

Sumo shifted his grip. Jon wheezed and coughed.

'Be sensible! Put him down before you hurt him. I know you're trying to get your friends out of trouble but if you carry on like this you'll get arrested.'

Sumo stared. 'There *are* plans though, aren't there, Prof? You and me know it. And that puts me one up on you, don't it? So, Janie, Kofi and Rorty, out here, now.'

Janie and I moved closer.

'Stay where you are,' said Quix.

'I've got recordings,' said Sumo. 'Of you and Col.'

Quix pressed his lips together. He drew in a long breath and pushed it out, noisily.

'You can have these two but not the hominin,' he said.

He was pushing us forward when there was a shout from outside. Two men came storming towards Sumo. They shoved him to the ground and prised open his arms. One scooped up Jon and headed straight back with him into the lab. He was charging through the doors when Janie shot past him screaming at the man outside to let Sumo go. The glass doors slid behind her and locked with a solid clunk.

Quix took a moment to gather his thoughts then narrowed his eyes. 'I want increased surveillance. All round the building. I want no more of this *flaming* nonsense and no more of these *interfering* kids. Call Jean to pick up Jon and put *him* in Lab One.'

He stormed off without even a glance in our direction.

I gave Jon a sneaky thumbs-up and Jon's eyes twinkled as he hid a little smile.

# 33

I have to hand it to Jon Quix. He has hidden talents. His performance with Sumo was outstanding; worthy of at least a Rising Star Award. But after the next drama he was, without question, heading for a BAFTA, quite probably Golden Globe material.

Minutes after his dad had left, the coughing fit began. There was no build-up to it. He went from cheerful to choking in milliseconds. The receptionist shot out from the front desk and by the time she'd reached him his eyes were bulging and his cheeks had turned ghostly white.

She screamed for someone called Dr Nam and as Dr Nam arrived Jon was taking great gulping breaths. In the next minute, two people were calling for an ambulance, Dr Nam was positioning Jon in readiness for the Heimlich manoeuvre and someone else had been sent for a scalpel. The receptionist was in tears.

The only reason I knew Jon was pretending was that in all the kerfuffle, I caught sight of his right hand waving a key card under Dr Nam's legs. No one saw me grab it. I backed away, sidled out of view and sprinted for Lab Three.

The key card took me through the first door. I stood in front of the cage. Rorty was stretched over the floor with his hands still tied and his eyes half-closed. I could see from the blood he'd been trying to remove the 3000 SS. The Hat was torn on one side. Maybe he'd knocked himself out.

'Rorty! Get up. You have to open the cage door.'

I watched his chest move up and down. He was taking short, shallow breaths.

There was a key-code panel. I tried punching in numbers. I didn't even know how many digits the code was.

'Rorty! Please! We haven't much time.'

I tried another set of numbers. A light on the panel started to flash. I heard an ambulance whining outside. I kicked at the bars. I stomped round the cage bashing and tugging. There was a plastic food box in a corner.

If I could throw things at him maybe he'd wake up. It was when I reached in and pulled the box aside that I saw the shapes.

Sticks of shrivelled carrot, sultanas, celery stalks, almonds and scraps of bread had been arranged across the floor to form a code: 74392K.

*Rorty, you're a genius!*

I entered the numbers on the keypad and the cage door clicked and released.

Gently, I lifted him. I stepped out of the cage, tugged open the lab door, pushing it wide with one foot, then headed down the corridor to find a fire exit.

Rorty's body was limp and awkward. I was sure he'd been drugged. I shifted him so his head and torso were over my shoulder. There were voices from nearby offices. There was shouting from outside. I ran to the end of the corridor, feeling Rorty's weight with every step. I kicked open a door which led to a staircase and in the corner was a doorway and a green sign. Tapping the card on a pad, I shouldered the door, shoved hard and stepped outside. I didn't even look, I just charged across the car park, gripping on to Rorty as his arms and head flopped and his legs crashed into mine.

'Behind the building, over the path. Behind the building, over the path,' I chanted as I ran.

Rain was spitting down and a plane roared overhead. I stomped through the trees, dodging the branches, trying to keep low, then crossed the cycle path to where Janie and Sumo were waiting.

None of us noticed the two bruisers keeping watch at the back.

'Quick, bring him over,' said Sumo. He was sitting astride the motorbike. The engine was running ready to go.

'Janie told you we didn't find Pogsy then?' I said.

'Yeah, so where is she?'

'We don't know.'

'I *detest* Quix,' said Janie. 'Absolutely *hate* him. But we're never giving up. We *will* find her. That's a total and absolute promise.'

'Come on then, little fella,' said Sumo. He lifted Rorty gently on to the bike.

'Hold him tight, won't you?' I said.

Sumo wrapped an arm around him and Rorty's eyes flickered like he was starting to wake up.

Sumo was edging the motorbike forward when we heard feet. Shoes on tarmac pounding in our direction.

In seconds, the first bruiser, Scowler, came smashing through the trees, shoved me to one side and tried to wrench Rorty from Sumo's arms. Still astride the bike, Sumo stood up and landed a heavy punch on the side of Scowler's jaw. Scowler paused for a second, looked Sumo in the eye, prised Sumo's hands off Rorty, then heaved him up and over his shoulder and took off with him through the trees back to the lab.

I didn't think. I just ran. I caught Scowler and launched myself on his back, locking my fists around his throat. He tried to break my grip but I held on and, reaching down, I tried to push the 3000 SS from Rorty's head.

'Wake up, Rorty, you've got to wake up!'

The Hat shifted a little, but not enough.

I was wrapping my legs around Scowler, trying to slow him down, when the second bruiser, Hefty, steamed over. Within seconds he'd ripped me clean off Scowler's back, dangled me in the air then dropped me like a piece of litter to the ground.

I could hear Janie screaming but Sumo's shouts were even louder and the sight of him powering across the car park, one arm in plaster, a bruised eye and a purple swollen lip, was terrifying. He barged straight into Hefty, who toppled and landed awkwardly on his elbow.

I thought I heard a crack as something broke, but that didn't stop Sumo. He ran straight for Scowler and floored him in seconds. Scowler fell heavily on his back. I quickly sat astride his legs and we both tried to pull Rorty from his grip.

'Do y'magic, Kofi,' yelled Sumo. 'Do y'deleting thing. Get rid of 'em.'

It didn't seem the right moment to tell him that it was Rorty who deleted things, not me.

Rorty's eyes flickered open. He looked around trying to take in what was happening. I snatched the Hat from his head.

'Rorty! Point and delete!'

But he was confused. He was still drowsy. I wasn't sure if he even recognised me and by this time another of Quix's men, Fists, was marching towards us.

Janie ran at him. She put her hands on his chest and tried to push him back. She stared straight at him and screamed:

'Don't you even dare!'

It was a brave thing to do but three bruisers against three kids wasn't a fair match. Ignoring Janie, Fists hauled Scowler to his feet, shoved Sumo aside and scooped Rorty off the floor.

'Give us the card,' he said. He held out his hand.

He meant the key card that Jon had given me to get out of the back door. I took it from my pocket and handed it over. I felt like I was boiling over, like I was going to explode with anger. I looked Fists straight in the eye.

'None of you have any idea what you're doing,' I shouted. 'You haven't a clue how important this hominin is to the world, do you? He's one of our ancient, ancient ancestors. And look what you're doing to him.'

It made no difference. The three of them just dusted themselves down, straightened their jackets and carried Rorty away.

'Just make sure you tell Professor Quix that he's not going to get away with this!' I yelled. 'Make sure you tell him that!'

We screamed. We roared. We stood there utterly helpless as they hauled Rorty back into Quix's lair.

I heard Rorty's faint cries.

The clunk of the closing door.

Then silence.

They'd got him.

# part three

# 34

Monday. School. Sumo, with one flabby buttock and a dinosaur thigh balanced on the edge of the desk. Stealth scrawling rude pictures on patches of spare plaster. Hammer admiring the fading cuts and bruises.

'Col the Neanderthal, hey?' he said.

'Yeah right,' said Sumo.

'Col the monster, hey?' Hammer threw a series of mock punches into the air.

'We'll get 'im,' said Stealth. 'All of us. Won't stand a chance. Pummel 'im to flaming pulp, we will.'

We wandered out of the classroom, down the steps and across to the language block. It was the fifteen-minute break between Maths and French. I felt a dark emptiness brewing inside me.

'Stupid, stupid, *stupid*!' I shouted.

Sumo rested a hand on my shoulder. 'In't your fault, Kofi. You got 'im out. In't your fault them thugs saw ya'.'

'It was *entirely* my fault. What was I thinking? Of course Quix would have blokes outside the lab. They were all over the place after you arrived with Jon. I'm such an idiot. Now we'll have no chance of getting back in. And they'll probably take him to the US or lock him in some underground bunker in Kazakhstan. And we'll never see him again.'

Janie came over. She put her arms around me. I could feel tears coming and tried to blink them away.

'If he's in the lab,' said Sumo, 'we've still got a chance. We've gotta get back in there and we've gotta get 'im out. You, me and Janie.'

They were the simplest words and they were all true. I looked at him, at his dark eyes peering out from little hoods of skin.

'You're right, Sumo,' I said. 'And that's exactly what we're going to do. We just have to work out how.'

Sumo looked down at his feet. 'Din't want to tell you before but there's more bad news.'

'Oh no,' said Janie.

'Got a dog on Sunday.'

I nodded, wondering why that was so bad.

'Present,' said Sumo.

'Yours?'

'Col's,' he said.

'Birthday?'

'Nah,' said Sumo.

'What sort?' I said.

'Golden retriever.'

'That's nice.'

Sumo scowled. 'Calling her Sniffy.'

'Great,' I said.

'I'm not s'posed to know but Quix gave it to Col.'

'What?'

'She's a proper sniffer dog.'

'You're kidding.'

'It's not just Col. Quix is fixing up other blokes with 'em, trained for drugs and stuff but they can sniff out anything. He asked Col coz they need the scent.'

'Pogsy's?' I said.

'They're using its blanket.'

'*Her* blanket,' said Janie.

'Yeah, I forgot,' said Sumo.

'What else did Quix say?'

'Something about dividing the team and searching in bits, starting at a one-mile something-or-other.'

'Radius?'

'Yeah, that were it.'

'Where were you when you heard all this?'

'Downstairs bog.' His face broke into a grin. 'Don't worry. They din't catch me.'

I kicked at the grass.

'Bad, in't it?' said Sumo.

'We've got to stop him. We've got to find a way.'

'Don't worry.' Sumo patted me on the shoulder. 'I've got a plan. You and me, right, we'll follow 'em and you'll pick 'em off, one by one, just blast 'em off the planet, you know, using y'magic and stuff, and we'll leave Col till last, get 'im really scared before you destroy the scumbag for good.'

I looked at him. 'This isn't *Call of Duty*, Sumo.'

'Yeah, well, I were just asking.'

'And if we kill everyone we won't find Rorty or Pogsy.'

'So we'll follow Col till Sniffy finds 'em, then we'll cull 'im.'

'Well let's see how it goes,' I said.

I drifted through lessons in a blur. I didn't answer questions. I wasn't even listening to what the teachers were saying. I spent most of the time just staring into space. Breeze came over and put her hand on my brow.

'You are not yourself today, young man.'

I shook my head.

'Do you want to talk about it?'

'No. No thanks, but it's nice of you to ask.'

She stood and watched me for a moment then moved closer. 'You know that anything you say will be confidential.'

'Yes,' I said.

'Even if it is about something happening outside of school.'

I looked at her. It was like she was reading my mind. 'Thank you. I know that.'

In the lunch break, Janie and I went to the library. Jon had asked us to meet up there. We huddled in a corner by the radiator.

'I wanted to send you a message but they might be tracking me,' Jon whispered.

'Who might be?'

'The people my dad's working with.'

'What did you hear?' said Janie.

'They're going to move him.'

A shock ran through me.

'I don't believe it,' said Janie.

Jon looked around nervously to check no one was near enough to overhear.

'When?' I whispered.

'Tonight.'

'What time?'

'Don't know. Sometime tonight.'

I grabbed Jon's jacket. 'Are you *absolutely* sure?'

'Yes. I heard my dad say it.'

'Where are they moving him to?' said Janie.

'I don't know.'

'Think,' I said. 'Any clues at all?'

'No,' said Jon.

'Did you hear anything else? Any other details?'

'N-nothing,' said Jon. His eyes were large and round. He looked terrified. 'If my dad knew I'd been listening I don't know what he'd do. I think he might actually kill me. Can you please let go of my jacket now?'

'Sorry,' I said. 'Sorry, Jon. Actually, you've done brilliantly. Thank you so much. We'll be there. We'll wait all night if we have to and we'll get him back. We'll bring him back home. That's an absolute promise.'

# 35

I think that
   maybe
   I should tell Mum and Dad about
      Rorty.

Things are getting Serious
      Big league
        Heavy.
And I am feeling
      Jittery
        Jumpy
          Jellified.

They've got him. They've snatched him away from us. Maybe they're going to do more experiments on him. Maybe they're going to expose him to the world.

I imagine him on talk shows.

And here he is!

The Amazing!

The Astonishing!

The Archaic!

Rorty Thrutch!

*So, Rorty, how d'you feel about being snatched from your jungle home where you and your kind have been living for the past 100,000 years and becoming mixed up in a mad scientist's scheme to take over the world?*

Because that's what is happening, isn't it? Rorty is a true relic of human evolution. An ancient artefact from an ancient lineage, living with us here on Planet Earth, who is in great danger. Our little friend from the forest who heads out into the night and brings back anything he likes because he's got two of Dad's chips in his brain that are doing all sorts of mixed-up stuff that no one thought was possible and no one would believe – not even Dad.

And MINDLINK's supposed to *help* people but Quix is turning it into a secret military weapon. Operation Silent Talk. Brain-to-brain communication. Deleting things just by pointing and clicking. How can he be so cruel? How can he steal my dad's work and turn it into something terrible? I bet he'll be on TV showing off with his great invention and be famous the world over.

And all you have, Rorty, is us to protect you. The Fantastic Four. It's like an adventure movie has plonked itself in the middle of boring old Bradborough with an all-star cast: the dashing young protagonist assisted by his resourceful feisty heroine, and the hefty, baddie-turned-goodie entrepreneur and the evil millionaire's wimpy son who turns out to be our secret weapon.

Things like this just don't happen in Bradborough postcode: N0 WH3R3.


Maybe
    I should go downstairs
    right now
    and tell them
    before
    it is
    too
    late.

# 36

Heart rate 92. Fingers visibly trembling. Sweat gathering on top lip. Needing the toilet every five minutes.

These are definite signs of being terrified.

The idea that later tonight I'd be hiding outside Quix's lab waiting for him and his bruisers to load Rorty into a vehicle of some sort, following them on Sumo's motorbike as they head off for some unknown destination and somehow intercepting them and rescuing Rorty, seemed totally and utterly crackers.

Who did I think I was? Alex flipping Rider?

And what if we didn't succeed? What if Quix managed to take Rorty away and experiment on him somewhere else? He needed two hominins for Operation Silent Talk. If finding Pogsy was too difficult, would he just go back to Rorty's island to get more of Rorty's family?

*We have to stop him.*

*We have no choice.*

There was one hour to go before I had to leave the house and meet up with Sumo. Dad appeared from his study. He looked tired and hungry.

'Come on,' he said. 'Mum's back late tonight. Let's take full advantage and have a fry-up. You chop the onions and tomatoes. I'll do the fish and the hot pepper sauce.'

He sliced plantain, grated fresh ginger, crumbled a couple of hot dried peppers and fried them in a deep pan.

We sat at the kitchen table with enough rice to feed the whole street and I thought, this would be a great time to see if he has any idea about Quix and the hominins. I felt my throat tightening and my heart kicking off again. I had to give him some information but not enough to plant the idea that Rorty and Pogsy might exist. After all, he did hear noises and had found Rorty's hair. I didn't want him to put hairs and hominins together.

'What if,' I started, 'for example, and this is a crazy, random, silly idea that I've just thought of, not relating at all to reality . . .'

Dad dipped a fish in the hot pepper. 'Go on,' he said.

'If there happened to be – and this is a bit like science fiction here – because, of course something like this could never *actually* happen . . .'

Dad looked at me over his glasses. He nodded encouragingly.

'What if there happened to be a sort of ancient species of human . . .' I paused to check his reaction. He was spooning a mountain of rice on to his plate. His expression didn't change, so I continued.

'. . . that was discovered alive, and a scientific researcher, or even, just for the sake of argument, someone like *you* implanted MINDLINK into the hominin's brain, would it be illegal? Would you be breaking the law?'

Dad loaded another teaspoon of pepper sauce on to the fish.

'If I was experimenting secretly on a creature as rare as an ancient human, without permission, I would be breaking every ethical code that ever existed. It would not only be illegal, but it would be immoral and would almost certainly land me in jail.'

'Good,' I said. 'Glad that's sorted then. Well, of course, if it was *you* that wouldn't be good at all, but good that you are so clear about the consequences of something that I completely made up and could never actually happen, in this day and age, or ever, in fact.'

I tucked into the fried plantain. I felt relieved that Quix would probably be locked up but sad that Jon might lose his dad.

Dad cleared his throat. 'Actually. I've been meaning to tell you.'

'Go on,' I said.

'We can't put MINDLINK into people.'

'What? Who says?'

'The health authorities. They're concerned the loss of memory will be long-term.'

'But it isn't.'

Dad looked up at me.

'Well. No. I mean, why should it be?'

'We have to demonstrate that. It hasn't been the case in the models we've used.'

'But they aren't human, are they?'

'They're the only ones we have to test MINDLINK.'

'Well I'm telling you, the memory loss is not permanent and you should continue your research and show the flipping authorities.'

Dad smiled. 'I wish it were so simple.'

'Look, Dad, the brain has to have time to adapt to having an electronic device attached to it. You have to do the tests for longer, that's all.'

Dad sighed. 'If only. We don't have the money, Kofi. It's pretty much case closed.'

He smiled again and placed his warm hand on mine. 'Let's finish this lot and clear up before Mum gets back.'

Dad put the extractor fan on full to get rid of the pepper smell and washed the frying pans. I wiped down the surfaces, several times, and sprayed lavender round the room.

Dad winked. 'She'll never know.'

I glanced at my watch. It was nearly time to go.

'I've . . . um . . . got to go out this evening,' I said, 'to a friend's . . . project stuff.'

I hated myself for telling a lie. I couldn't even look Dad in the face but it was a lie for a good reason. I hoped he'd understand.

'It might be quite late,' I said.

'How late?'

'Not sure.'

'Planning on staying over?'

'Might be.'

'Then leave a phone number and address and let me know what you decide. What's the project on?'

'Our ancient ancestors.'

Dad smiled. 'I see, so that's why you were asking about MINDLINK. Taking your aluminium hat with you?'

'Nah. Don't need that any more,' I said.

# 37

The trees at the edge of the car park gave us cover as night fell. We'd been taking turns to keep watch. Jon had been on the first shift until he had to catch the bus home, then it was Janie's turn with her binoculars and a takeaway pizza. And now, at seven in the evening, it was Sumo and me hiding in the shadows with a full view of two sides of Quix's lab.

'Got 'em scared, 'aven't we?' whispered Sumo.

'Hope so,' I said.

'Good job mi mam's not on lates tonight. Wouldn't have been able to come.'

'Doesn't Col look after Shima?'

'Nah. Remember what I told ya? He's a thug. Monster. That's why you're gonna get rid of 'im, aren't ya? Anyhow he's busy training Sniffy. Getting her used to Pogsy's smell before they hunt for her.'

I felt a shiver right through me.

We were dressed in black. Sumo had even brought his shades to look like a real undercover agent until he realised they weren't going to be that helpful in the dark. Sections of the building and car park were lit with spotlights and there were streetlamps along the cycle path behind the trees. The entrance to the lab was as bright as a shop window, with all the light from indoors spilling out over the steps, but the boundary where we were was dark and secluded. Behind us, next to the fence was the motorbike, Sumo's backpack and two helmets.

We fell quiet as one of Quix's men, Scowler, strolled along the back of the building. He'd been circling the lab every fifteen minutes, checking the back door, scanning the car park and coming uncomfortably close to get a good view of the roof.

'Jumpy, aren't they?' whispered Sumo.

'Yeah,' I breathed.

'He's still got that bruise where I punched 'im.'

'Yeah. That's probably not a good thing,' I said.

All the nerves I'd felt earlier had gone. Even though we had no idea what Quix was going to do, somehow I was sure we'd succeed. We'd get Rorty back. We had to.

*We're coming for you*, I said to him in my head. *We're coming to rescue you.*

Hefty had now joined Scowler outside. They kept checking their phones. At eight o'clock a white van pulled up at the door where I'd escaped with Rorty just two days ago.

Sumo sat up. 'Here we go,' he whispered.

Hefty swung open the van doors. There was a mesh cage inside, the sort you'd use to transport animals.

'Get ready to start the bike,' I whispered, 'but only when they're in the van and heading for the gate.'

'Wilco,' said Sumo.

The back door opened and Fists appeared with Rorty in his arms. My heart thumped.

'He looks more awake,' I whispered. 'But he's still wearing the Hat.'

Fists pushed Rorty into the cage and locked it with a key, then headed back inside the lab, leaving the van doors still open. Scowler got into the driving seat and seemed to be checking the sat nav. Hefty marched around the corner to the side of the building talking to someone on his phone.

In that moment no one was watching Rorty.

Without hesitation I was on my feet powering around

the fringes of the car park in the shadows. I edged along the building and crouched by the cage.

'Rorty,' I whispered. He was slumped to one side but his eyes flickered open. 'Pull the Hat off.'

He shuffled a little to show that his hands were tied behind his back.

'Move closer.' I glanced up to see if Scowler had heard me or if Hefty was on his way back, but they were both still distracted. 'Put your head on the bars so I can touch you.'

His heavy head tilted sideways. I dug into the foil until there was a small hole just above his scar so MINDLINK could work.

'See if you can delete the cage door,' I breathed. 'Turn round and try to draw a circle.'

Rorty twisted but he struggled to point at the bars and could only make small movements with his hands.

'Click and think delete.'

Rorty was scrunching up his face in concentration when I heard someone marching towards the van. I sank to the ground, rolled towards the building and stayed very still in the shadows. Hefty slammed the van door shut and got into the front seat, then the engine hummed into life and they pulled off.

Within seconds, Sumo was spinning the motorbike across the car park and tossing me a helmet. I jumped on the back and grabbed hold of the seat. Stealthily, we edged along behind the van as it turned into the main road.

I couldn't believe I'd almost got him back and now we had no idea where they were going to take him.

It took me a while to work out that the white van was heading for Little Crompton-on-Leigh, not a port or a private airfield miles away. I'd thought Quix could be moving Rorty to another country, somewhere where he could disappear and never be found again. I didn't think they'd be heading back to his house.

The van sped along narrow twisting roads. Every now and then the motorbike headlight lit up the back of the van and I tried to see if Rorty had managed to make a hole in the door, but it was too dark to see properly.

'Keep your distance,' I shouted to Sumo. 'Don't want them to think they're being followed.'

We pulled back along a straight stretch of road and watched the rear lights of the van disappear round the next corner. Sumo slowed even more but after two more bends we pulled up at a junction and couldn't see the van any more.

'Lost 'em,' he shouted.

I grabbed my phone, opened my sat nav and punched in Jon's address. But what if they weren't going to Quix's house? I just had to hope I was right.

'Turn left,' I said to Sumo. He accelerated so fast that I almost fell backwards. 'Now right,' I shouted and we leaned into the corner as the bike sped around a curve.

The country road became a tunnel of overhanging branches. It was pitch black apart from the shivering beam of the headlight marking our way. We headed down and down a dark narrow hill that seemed to go on for ever. Grass stems snagged our legs and water splashed over us from deep ruts in the road. We were heading up the other side when I heard the noise. Helicopter blades chopping through the night air.

'Can you hear that?' I shouted.

Sumo pointed at the bright white light high above the village.

'It's another mile,' I said. 'Get moving!'

Sumo accelerated and I tightened my grip on the seat.

'Another right turn and we should be in the village,' I said.

We turned down the main street of Little Crompton-on-Leigh. It was packed with cars on either side and we had to slow as a gaggle of pub-goers crossed the road. There was no sign of the helicopter now. It must have landed. As soon as the road was clear again, Sumo accelerated. We tore past thatched cottages and late-night dog walkers then turned into the narrow lane that led to Quix's house. We pulled up just in time to see the gates of the Manor House closing and the rear lights of the white van disappearing down the driveway.

And beyond, on Professor Quix's brightly lit lawns, were the enormous spinning blades of the helicopter, waiting to take Rorty away.

# 38

We couldn't get in through the Manor House gate.

'Go round!' I shouted.

Sumo heaved the bike back on to the road and we hurtled down the lane. We stopped in front of a metal gate leading to the fields where Rorty had deleted Quix's dogs. I got off the bike and pulled back the bolt for Sumo to ride in.

We sped towards the side of the field that led to Quix's garden. The bike tossed us from side to side as the tyres caught in ruts and bumps. There was a chain around Quix's gate so I hopped off the bike thinking we'd have to climb over. But Sumo had other ideas. Like Robin Hood drawing an arrow from his quiver, he reached into his backpack and pulled out a huge pair of bolt cutters. He sliced through the chain with one cut and bumped the gate open with a heavy kick.

The lawns, which had been covered with two marquees and a bouncy castle only a week before, were as bright as daylight. Spotlights beamed down from the steps and the patio. The helicopter blades were still spinning. The noise drowned out the sound of the motorbike as we tore across the grass to the side of the house. I scrambled off the bike, sprinted to the driveway and pulled open the doors of the white van. The cage was empty but there was a small hole in the steel mesh that wasn't there before. Only one smart little hominin could have done that.

Sumo thundered up behind me. He grabbed my coat. 'Come on, or they'll be taking off and that'll be it.'

We powered round the front of the Manor House, past the front door, along the path and turned down the side. We edged along the wall and crouched as we looked out over the back lawn. There were four men in black suits loading holdalls into the helicopter. Professor Quix was shouting at the pilot.

'Where is he?' said Sumo.

'Probably in the helicopter already.'

Sumo shook his head. 'No point hiding then. If we don't do nothing, he'll be gone for ever.'

I imagined at least three horrible endings in the space of three seconds. I was so scared I could hardly move.

'Wait,' I said.

'No waiting, Kofi. We're going. Now.'

Sumo shoved me from the shadowy wall out into the bright light. I felt his firm hand on my back as we went down the steps on to the lawn. Immediately two men in black suits ran over. We didn't struggle. There was no point.

'Ah!' Quix screeched and screwed up his face. He strode towards us and yelled over the noise of the whirring blades. 'What the hell are you doing here?' He threw his hands in the air. 'Haven't you got it yet? This has nothing to do with you. Stop interfering!' He turned to the men gripping our arms. 'Just get them as far away from me as possible.'

Sumo twisted and kicked, trying to get free.

'Wait!' I yelled. 'Professor Quix, please, just one last request.'

He turned.

'Rorty's been our friend all this time, Professor Quix, sir, we really care about him and if it's all right with you, we just wanted to say one last goodbye.' I gave Sumo a side glance. He'd managed to produce a genuine tear which was rolling down his cheek. 'Just a goodbye hug. Please, Professor Quix, before you take him away.'

Quix scrunched up his face. He shook his head. He closed his eyes and gestured towards the house.

Rorty wasn't in the helicopter. Not yet anyway. Hefty was pushing him slowly down the steps. The Hat was tied to his head. His hands were bound behind his back and there was a thick cord around his ankles.

I felt like I was imploding.

The other four men were getting ready to climb on board. I could see the pilot in the cockpit. The noise of the engine was getting louder.

Sumo sidestepped next to me and pressed something into my hands. It felt like a pair of thick scissors. I pushed them up my sleeve as I walked over to Rorty.

'It's time to say goodbye,' I said.

Rorty looked up at me with great sorrowful eyes. 'Is Kofi. Is brother.'

I put my arms around him and felt the cord binding his hands. 'There's so much I want to say, but so little time before you go.' I closed the scissors and felt them slice easily through the cord.

'Come on!' yelled Quix. 'You're wasting time and money!'

242

I turned to speak directly into Rorty's ear to make sure he heard me.

'Your hands are free. Do something spectacular.'

I stepped away and for a few moments Rorty stood there, frozen with his hands behind his back, staring at the helicopter. Then slowly, he brought his right hand forward and pointed. The huge machine started to rock from side to side. Quix ran towards it, jumping up and down, waving his arms and shouting. The four men and the pilot quickly scrabbled to the door and jumped out. Quix's face was crimson with anger. He yelled at Hefty, who'd been escorting Rorty.

'Get hold of his arms! Stop him!'

But Hefty was rooted to the spot, in shock. Quix bolted across the grass, heading straight for us.

Rorty paused and drew in a deep breath, then in one incredible movement he raised his right hand again and, with finger and thumb outstretched, aimed at the helicopter, and slowly drew his fingers together.

Until that moment, no one in the history of the world had ever seen a helicopter shrink. The noise of the blades and the engine faded as it grew smaller and smaller to about a quarter of its size. Quix turned and screeched. Some of the men ran, others just stood there unable to believe what they were seeing. Before Quix had time to turn on us, I scooped Rorty into my arms and ran with Sumo to the motorbike.

'Holy Moly!' shouted Sumo. 'It's not you, is it? It's Rorty who's the flipping magician!'

I cut the cord binding Rorty's feet and we jumped on to the bike. I gave one last glance behind and saw Jon's pale face at the window. He was smiling.

We raced back over the lawns and field, through the gate and out on to the road. I pulled Rorty close like I'd never let him go again. The bike sped along the country lanes and we laughed and howled and whooped as loud as we could.

We reached Boxgrove Drive around ten-thirty. We stepped on to the pavement, took off our helmets and hugged each other.

'Total awesomeness,' said Sumo. He shook his head. 'Look at mi hands.'

'Look at mine,' I said.

We were both still trembling.

Sumo knelt in front of Rorty. 'That was the best magic I've ever seen. D'you know how much we could make if you were on TV? Now listen, little fella, from now on, just keep clear of that Quix guy, all right?

Don't think we can go through that again. Mi nerves are in shreds.'

Rorty's eyes were large and round. He looked exhausted.

I hugged Sumo again. 'You were magnificent,' I said. 'Couldn't have done it without you.'

'Piece o' cake,' said Sumo. 'Best thing I've done in ages.'

'Now all we have to do now is find Pogsy before the dogs do.'

Sumo patted me on the back. 'We'll do it,' he said. 'After tonight we can do flipping anything.'

We all hugged again and Sumo took off on his bike, waving all the way. Then Rorty made a hole in the house wall and we crept quietly upstairs.

He stayed with me that night. It was too late and too dark to trudge over the Burrows to Heron's Island. I whispered to Mum and Dad that I was back then lay awake for ages looking at the stars through my window.

At 2:17 a.m. my phone buzzed. It was a text from Sumo.

**Colz starting the search 2morrow**

The dogs were ready to hunt for Pogsy.

I didn't sleep at all after that.

# 39

Tuesday. 11:15 a.m.

'I've seen Col's map,' said Sumo.

'Oh yeah? What's on it?'

'A circle round town, one-mile radius, with your house bang in the middle. Six blokes. Six dogs. Six pieces. Like a pizza.'

'Good job Rorty's on Heron's Island,' I said.

'Yeah,' said Sumo. 'By the way, you're looking knackered.'

'So are you,' I said, laughing.

We were in Breeze's class that afternoon. She told us that Mr Steele had been so impressed by our work on Origins that he wanted us to make a display in the assembly hall.

'But before I reveal the plans,' she said, 'let's hear the final presentations.'

Sumo was the last to go. He eased himself out of the chair and hitched up his trousers. He collected his papers and lumbered between desks to stand at the front. He glanced at Hammer, who was pulling faces, so he looked to the floor whilst he gathered himself.

'Starting off, I hadn't a clue what I was gonna to do mi project on. I didn't know nothing 'bout origins, or nothing. I didn't know nothing 'bout genes or ancient ancestors but I do now coz Kofi told me. Then when I heard Jez talk about his family in Pakistan and seeing photos of him and his granddad, I thought I'd try look for mi dad, coz I haven't got a dad, not a proper one anyhow.

'I asked mi mam what his name was. I'd never asked her before. She didn't want to know at first, she was cross with me asking. Then suddenly like, when she was feeding Shima, she just said it, like that. Bapak Suparman. And I said, are you sure? Like Superman? And she said yeah, 'cept you spelt it different, and then she smiled, which wasn't like her really.

'So I thought that was a good start having a dad called Superman and I looked everywhere to find out

247

about him and I found his name comes from Indonesia. And it all made sense then coz mi middle name's from Indonesia. I told Mam that there's more than seventeen thousand islands and she said I'd better start looking then. She's getting a bit of a joker is mi mam.

'But how d'you find one Bapak Suparman in two hundred and sixty million people? I said. And then she had a think about it. She sat with her eyes closed and I could see them moving behind her eyelids like she was shining little lights in the corners of her head. Then she told me he worked on a ship. A ship that brought wood to England. And I said, where did you meet? And she said, where's the most romantic city in England? And I said, I've no idea, and she said, Hull of course.

'So I wrote this email to the person in charge of the port in Hull. I said,

'*Dear Person in charge of Hull port, I'm looking for my dad. His name is Bapak Suparman and he works on a ship that brings wood from Indonesia. I've never met him before but I'd like to. He knows my mam. She's called Sheila. I'm thirteen now. From Sebastien Lombok Fitzgerald. P.S. Lombok is an island in Indonesia.*

'They took ages to answer.'

Sumo paused to take a piece of paper from his pocket. He unfolded it.

'Got this yesterday.

'*Dear Mr Sebastien Lombok Fitzgerald,*

*Thank you for your enquiry. Unfortunately, we do not hold records of all crew members on incoming cargo vessels. We are very sorry to disappoint you. We wish you every success in locating your father.*'

The room was silent. No one knew what to say.

After a long pause Breeze said, 'Thank you, Sebastien. Don't give up, will you? I'm sure you'll find him. Just don't give up.'

Sumo nodded.

'Yeah,' he said. 'Yeah, I'll keep looking coz he's mi dad, in't he? He's mi real dad. Mi real origins.'

# 40

Wednesday. 3:45 p.m.

'Breeze has a car seat,' said Janie.

'Interesting.' I yawned.

'It's more than interesting. She doesn't have kids.'

'Haven't we been through this before?'

'Yes, but that was about nappies.'

'Well, maybe she's adopted a baby. Or maybe she's helping out a friend whose car has broken down and needs to get her kid to the nursery.'

'What, the friend who needed nappies?'

'How do I know?' I said.

Janie huffed. 'Well listen to this then. I've just seen her getting into her car, which is when I noticed the car seat and she was screeching into her mobile saying "what sort of dogs?", "in the back garden?", "what do

250

you mean frenzied?", then she said, "OK, OK, I'm coming. Tell them we're calling the police." '

'Dogs?' I looked at her. 'Number one, Breeze doesn't screech and number two, why didn't you say that in the first place?'

Janie scowled.

'Someone's had an extra serving of crabby today. Old crabby-pants.'

'Where does she live?'

'No idea.'

'This is serious,' I said. 'Use your phone. White pages dot co dot uk. Enter Ndiaye.'

We shot out of school. We didn't know which way to go. We hurried up Longlin Lane.

'N-d-i-a-y-e,' I said.

Janie paused while she entered the name.

'Seventeen Leakey Close. Off Glaston Avenue.'

The ancient maroon Volvo estate had been abandoned in the road. The driver's door hung open. Several white-haired neighbours were gathered on the pavement. We heard Breeze's voice.

'This is *my* house. This is *my* compound. You have *no* right to be here.'

We heard a dog barking as we edged up the drive. It was Col and Sniffy and another bloke and another dog.

'We're plain-clothes police,' we heard Col say. 'These are highly trained detection dogs.'

'Show me your identification,' said Breeze.

Col folded his arms. 'If you would like to accompany me to the patrol car, I will,' he said.

'I am not accompanying you anywhere. There is no reason to be searching my property.'

'We believe you are harbouring an illegal immigrant.'

There was a pause.

'Thing is, we know you're hiding someone in there, they don't miss nothing these dogs. So let's just walk inside, do the search, or do we have to make a forced entry?'

'Forced entry will not be necessary, Mr Fitzgerald,' I said.

Col whipped round. His eyes were bulging. His face was flushed. There was a glimmer of recognition.

I waved Janie's phone at him.

'Just had Detective Darwin on the line, Bradborough CID. He's tells me there are no sniffer dogs working in the area and certainly no plain-clothes police with authorisation to enter a property at seventeen Leakey Close. They're sending an officer round as we speak.'

Col's mate glanced at Col, then back at me. They muttered something between them. Sniffy lay down and rested her head on her paws. It seemed ages before anyone moved.

*I have to do something*, I thought. *They're not actually going to go unless I do something.*

'I know where your stuff is,' I said, looking at Col.

He scowled. He jabbed a finger at me. 'Wait a minute. I know you. Seb's class. What d'you mean, my stuff?'

'The stuff in your garage.'

Col's face tightened and reddened. 'Did *you* nick it? Did *you* nick my garage?'

'No, no,' I said. 'I just know where the stuff is, so if you want it back you have to leave now, immediately, without another word, and I'll get it back for you. All of it. But you have to go now. No fuss.'

I saw the alarm in their eyes. I watched them muttering to each other.

'You're lying,' said Col.

'No I'm not. Ask Miss Ndiaye. She's my teacher.'

Breeze looked slightly confused, but she nodded. 'I would believe him if I were you. He will keep his word about the *stuff* but you better leave before the real police arrive. He wasn't lying about that either.'

Col glared. He snapped at Sniffy's lead and swore under his breath.

'Bunch of idiots,' he said. 'You've got something in that house and you know it. We know it. Don't be surprised if you have another visit. Sooner than you think. And *you* . . .' he said, jabbing a finger in my direction, 'can be expecting a visit from me very soon.'

They took off down the drive. Sniffy tugged and yelped as they passed Breeze's car but Col yanked her back and growled at her and they stormed out of Leakey Close.

We were silent for a time. Breeze sat on the steps by her front door. She closed her eyes and breathed deeply.

'OK,' she said, looking up again. 'How on earth are you two mixed up in this?'

She didn't invite us in. We sat on the steps with glasses of lemonade and a plate of shortbread. A couple of concerned neighbours came and went.

Janie explained. 'I saw you in the school car park and I heard you talking about dogs and saw you rushing off. I told Kofi. We were worried.'

'Hmm,' said Breeze. 'Thank you for your concern but there really was no need.' She looked at each of us. She didn't smile.

'And how, young man, do you happen to know where this *stuff* is? Stolen, I assume?'

I looked at her. There was no point lying but there was no chance she'd believe the truth.

'Miss Ndiaye,' I said. 'Can you trust me?'

She considered me for some moments. 'Yes,' she nodded. 'I can.'

'I promise that when all this is over I will tell you everything. Janie and I will tell you everything. We haven't done anything wrong or illegal. It's just that, it's such an astonishing story that you wouldn't believe it right now.'

Breeze smiled. A wide full smile that made little dimples in her cheeks. 'Then I will wait, young man. I love astonishing stories.'

'Thank you,' said Janie. 'Thank you so much. You're such a brilliant teacher you know. Such an inspiration. We didn't want anything . . .'

Janie stopped. She glanced at me then back at Breeze.

'But don't you find it strange that the dogs smelt someone in your house?'

Breeze shrugged. 'They just wanted to snoop around. Maybe they heard about my valuable collection of stone tools.'

'Really?' said Janie.

Breeze laughed.

'You should report them to the police,' I said. 'In case they come back.'

'Yes. Maybe. But I would rather forget about it now.'

We brushed the crumbs from our laps. We thanked her for the drinks and headed for the gate.

We called, 'See you tomorrow,' and in the quiet that followed I thought I heard the sound of a baby crying.

'Goodbye, Detective Darwin,' she called back. 'First name Charles, I suppose.'


We walked in silence to the end of Leakey Close.

'Are you thinking what I'm thinking?' I said.

'You're thinking Pogsy's in there, aren't you?'

I nodded.

'And a baby?' Janie whispered.

I stood there trying to take it in.

'We've got to go back and ask her,' said Janie.

We were heading up to Breeze's again when my mobile rang. It was Sumo.

'I've got to get out of the house.' He sounded terrified and breathless.

'What's up?'

'Col's gone ballistic.'

'Oh no.'

'Can I bring Shima round?'

'Yeah. Yeah course.'

I started to run. 'Emergency. We've got to help Sumo. Breeze will have to wait.'

# 41

Wednesday. 4:55 p.m.

Sumo came up to my room. Shima's nappy needed changing.

'Best in the bathroom.' I nudged him towards the door.

'Where do I chuck this?' he said, a few minutes later, swinging a little bag.

'Bin outside. I'll show you.'

Mum came in as we were closing the back door.

'Oh. Hello.' She looked surprised to see us all there.

'Hullo. I'm Sebastien. Pleased to meet ya. This is mi half-sister, Shima.'

'She's lovely,' said Mum. 'How old is she?'

'Four'n'half months. Give or take.'

Mum smiled and stroked her fingers.

'She's a big girl for her age.'

'Takes after mi mam.'

I steered Sumo through the lounge. He was still a bit shaky. Janie followed.

'Let's take her in the garden,' I said. 'She'll like it there.'

We went out on to the patio and I slid the door closed behind us. We sat on the wooden chairs. Sumo's brow was glistening and little beads of sweat were shining in the groove above his lip.

'He's smashed mi door in,' he said. 'He smashed mi bed an' everything. He smashed Shima's cot. I heard him on the mobile saying they got a scent at Breeze's house but you messed it up and he's coming after you for his stuff. What's goin' on?'

'Coming here?'

'Yeah. That's why I called you. Did you do something with that garage or not?'

I looked at him. 'It was Rorty,' I said.

'And it's him that's got all the TVs and computers and mobiles?'

'Yes,' I said. I took out my phone.

**URGENT. Copy Col's stuff in the garage. Put it on the bank by Heron's Island. Stay hidden. Sumo and I are coming with Col. Confirm you have received this.**

'You'll have to leave Shima with my mum,' I said.

'Right,' said Sumo.

'Janie, can you stay with Mum? Stop her panicking?'

Janie nodded. 'OK, but what are you going to do?'

'We'll wait for Col then take him through the Burrows.'

'Right,' said Sumo. 'Good plan.'

'That's not a good plan,' said Janie. 'That's a terrifying plan.'

I told Mum to lock the front and back doors.

'What on earth for?' she said.

'There's something we have to sort out.'

'That doesn't explain why I have to lock the doors.'

'Please, Mum. We haven't much time. I promise I'll tell you about it later.'

Mum bunched her face into a tight scowl. 'What's this about, Kofi?'

'I can't say right now. You have to trust me. Please, Mum.'

'All right.' She sighed and nodded as Sumo placed Shima gently in her arms. 'But I want a full explanation when you're back.'

We went outside. I checked my phone but there was no response. We heard Shima crying. We saw Mum jigging her about in the lounge and Janie biting her nails. We peered up and down the street.

'He'll be coming,' said Sumo. 'He was like a pit bull when I left. He could kill us both you know. With 'is bare hands.'

My heart started to race. I looked at my phone again. *Come on, Rorty, come on.*

A car pulled up. Heavy metal throbbed from inside. Col got out and slammed the door. He saw us waiting.

'Get in,' he said.

'What for?'

'Shut up and get in.'

'We can't get your stuff by car.'

Col put his hands on his hips. The dark clefts between his eyebrows deepened.

'I'll show you the way,' I said. 'It's across the Burrows.'

He pointed his key fob at the car. The lights flashed. I led them round the back of the house. I glanced at Mum standing with Shima at the kitchen window.

*Stay where you are*, I said to her in my head. *It'll be all right. Stop fussing. We'll be OK.*

Across the grass, past the shed and Mum's butterfly meadow and through the garden gate. We trudged past the pile of building bricks and hardened cement. The Burrows looked strangely grey and sinister.

Col stopped suddenly and grabbed my shoulder. He glared right into me. 'If this is a wind-up, you're history.'

'It's not,' I said.

I glanced at my phone. Nothing.

We reached the bend in Burrows brook. I remembered taking the Molimo there under the stars and the moon and the planets. Where was my starman now?

*Don't let me down, Rorty. I need you now, more than ever.*

Along the hedges, around the fields. Sumo was lagging behind, flushed and breathless. Col and I waited for him to catch up.

'Has he something to do with this?' said Col.

'No,' I said. 'He knows absolutely nothing.'

'So how did you get all my stuff over these fields, on your tod?'

'You're going to find out,' I said. 'Very soon.'

'Am I now?' He took hold of my shoulders and shook me. 'These hands and these arms have made people disappear, never to be found again. These hands and these arms have dug graves. Get what I'm saying?'

'Yes,' I said.

He shoved me in the back and I started walking again.

*Come on, Rorty. Please, Rorty. Not far now. Follow the river. Along the bank until we see the great willow. The stuff should be here. It should be on the bank by the grassy edge where we launched the dinghy.*

Col stood with his hands on his hips. He swiped the sweat trickling down his temples.

There was no sign of it. No stolen TVs. No boxes of smartphones.

'Wait here,' I said. I went beyond the tree. I searched the bushes and the swampy reeds.

I looked at my phone. No signal.

I yelled. 'Rorty!'

I put my hands to my mouth. I screamed.

'Rorty!'

Col and Sumo stood on the bank watching.

'Let me look round the other side,' I said.

Col took hold of me.

'You're going nowhere, mate.' He pressed his face into mine. He pushed me backwards and shoved me to the ground.

'It's on the island. I just remembered. Your stuff's on the island there. Tell him, Sumo. Tell him it's true.'

Col shook his head.

'Time's up, mate. You've messed up, haven't ya? Messed up the monkey hunt. Lied about my stuff. Brought old Col here for no good reason. Got Col a bit cross, haven't ya? Got Col a bit wound up.'

He glanced down. He was loosening a rock half buried in the ground. He tugged it from the earth. He pounded it from one hand to the other.

'Don't, Col,' said Sumo. 'He's mi mate, he hasn't done nothing wrong.'

Clouds drifted across the sun. There was a sudden clattering of wings and the grating calls of magpies. They rose from Heron's Island and scattered over the trees. Then a deeper shadow, something passing over us.

'Move!' yelled Sumo.

I rolled and scrambled to my feet. I saw Sumo powering towards me, felt him grabbing my arm, propelling me to the bank, to the edge of the river. We toppled over each other.

Dark objects were falling from the sky. The first landed just a metre from Col. It thudded to the ground. Col jumped to one side and looked up as another plummeted towards him. It crashed and the box broke open, ejecting shards of glass just missing his legs. A smaller object caught his shoulder. Col started to run. He took two or three strides then stopped as if he'd hit a wall. He strained to move. He fell forward. He grabbed at the grass, dug his boots into the earth, but something, someone, didn't want him to leave. Stretched out on the ground, Col was slowly being dragged back towards the river.

'What's going on?' he roared.

A Samsung 51-inch, with two 10-watt speakers and an internal menu of twenty-nine European languages, descended slowly. It fell to within inches of Col's face and hovered. Col was still pinned to the ground. He tried to move. He used his arms to push but he couldn't budge. The TV tilted and came to rest over Col's head.

Other boxes arrived in procession like an aerial conveyor belt. Each one was brought down carefully and added to the heap. Ten thousand quid's worth of stolen goods gradually enclosed Col's body.

'This is mad!' said Sumo. He looked at me sidelong. 'So Rorty made the garage disappear and he came into Deft's class, invisible like, and painted my face and did the clown at the party?'

I nodded.

Sumo grinned. He nudged me. 'And all that time, you let me think it were you?'

'I said it wasn't me. But if I'd told the truth you wouldn't have believed me, would you?'

'Probably not. So where's the garage now?'

'On the island.'

'How did it get there?'

'That's another thing. When he makes stuff disappear, like deleting something, he can bring it back.'

Sumo smirked. He started to laugh. He lay on his back and covered his face and his whole body shook. He sat up again with tears in his eyes.

'You know what this means, don't ya?' he said. He cocked his head in Col's direction. He'd almost disappeared under the mound of stuff from the garage.

'I'm not sure, Sumo. A garage is one thing but I don't know about something alive. Rorty deleted Quix's dogs but he's never tried to bring them back. We don't know if they'd survive.'

Sumo shrugged. 'Does it matter? Does it matter with a thug like him if he never comes back?'

If it wasn't for Janie, Dad might never have found out about Rorty. Mum phoned him after she'd seen Col.

She mentioned 'tattoos' and 'gangster-like qualities' and Dad left a departmental meeting to come straight home. Janie told him that we'd be near Heron's Island and came with him to show him the way.

Rorty finally appeared. My text hadn't reached him because the signal was weak, so he didn't know we were in trouble until he heard me shouting. We asked him if he could restore one of the dogs that he'd deleted at Jon's party. To see if it was possible. To know if it would come back alive.

Rorty stood still. His eyeballs flickered behind his eyelids. He gave a deep click and spread his hands. Instantly four dogs were writhing and yelping in front of us. In the confusion, they turned on each other, snapping at tails and ears.

Rorty scrabbled up the willow tree. Sumo and I tried to calm them down.

'Heel!' I shouted.

'Come here, y'stupid hounds.'

They still had collars and leashes. We ran round trying to catch hold of them. Sumo stamped on one lead, jolting an Alsatian to a halt, but it bared its teeth and lowered its head and when Sumo turned to run, it took off with the others over the fields.

We didn't see Col inching his way out from under the heap. We didn't notice anything until the boxes tumbled and crashed.

Dad and Janie were powering down the sloping field to the riverbank, all arms and elbows and leaping strides. They were fifty metres away when Col came for us. There was a gash in his head and a trail of blood down his face. He screeched and ran straight at us. We just stood there, petrified.

I glimpsed Rorty's outline in the tree. I saw his hand pointing at Col.

'Sumo, say goodbye to your stepdad,' I whispered.

And that was it. In the blink of an eye, Mr Colin Fitzgerald was no more.

# 42

Wednesday. Sometime after 7:00 p.m.

The tin of home-made ginger nuts lay open on the patio table. Extra chairs had been brought from the garage. Janie called her mum to say she'd be home late and Shima lay fast asleep in Sumo's arms.

'I'm trying to take this all in,' said Dad. He was standing with his eyes tightly closed and his index fingers pressed to his temples. 'You're telling me that there really *is* another species of human?'

'Yes,' I said.

'A *hominin*?'

'Yes,' I said.

'And there are two of them here in Bradborough?'

'We think so,' I said.

'And the male has a MINDLINK implant?'

'Two, according to Professor Quix.'

Dad's mouth opened slightly. '*Two?*'

'They've been implanted for at least eight weeks. Rorty had a bit of memory loss at the beginning but he can remember everything now.'

A smile spread across Dad's face.

'That's why you shouldn't give up, Dad. MINDLINK really works.'

Mum was staring right through me. Her mouth was open and she was breathing quickly.

'Who is this Professor Quix?' she said. 'How has he got your chips, George? Do you know him?'

'Not yet,' said Dad. He turned to me again. 'So let's get this straight. This Quix chap must have stolen the plans to build MINDLINK, implanted two of them, and together they have enabled invisibility, molecular replication and telekinesis?'

'Amongst other things,' I said.

'Woo,' said Dad. His eyes were wide and staring. 'If I hadn't witnessed it myself I would not have believed it.'

'What did you see?' said Mum.

'Things I did not think were possible. Things outside the natural laws of physics.'

'Good God,' gasped Mum. 'What does he look like, this hominin?'

'Dad didn't see him,' I said. 'Rorty was camouflaged.'

Mum's eyes shifted from Dad to me.

'Is he the . . .?'

'Illiterate with the bag of biscuit wrappers? Yes,' I said.

'And the hut?'

'Yes. He built that himself.'

'Who else knows?' said Mum.

'Only a handful of people. But I don't think they *really* know. I mean, they don't know the real truth about him.'

The story gradually unravelled. We all told little bits of it. Weird bits. Completely barmy bits. All of it true. All of it unbelievable.

'In this house. Since March?' said Mum.

'Sorry,' I said. 'It was a humanitarian crisis.'

'A 3000 SS Turbo?' said Dad. 'I quite fancy one of those myself.'

'Do you know how much we've spent on aluminium foil?' said Mum. 'It's four pounds for a ten-metre roll in Tesco's.'

We nibbled more biscuits and drained our cups. Then silence fell and darkness enclosed us. Mum tucked her feet on the chair and hugged her knees.

'It feels like the world's just tilted,' she said. 'Like we've experienced a tectonic shift and everything we assumed, everything we believed, is no longer true.'

Dad put his arm around her. 'And these three have been trying to deal with all this on their own.'

Mum nodded. She smiled. 'Where's the female?'

I glanced at Janie. 'She's called Pogsy,' I said. 'She's still missing.'

'Does she have MINDLINK?'

'No. They must have escaped before Quix had time to implant it in her. Rorty has something called a Molimo. It has mysterious powers that'll draw Pogsy to us.'

'Oh it has,' said Janie. 'It's like music but much, much more. It's like being possessed in your heart and in your head and your whole body. Voices, feelings and something else, something there isn't a word for. They've been on roundabouts in the night.'

'*Who* have been on roundabouts?' said Mum.

'Me and Rorty,' I said, and I knew I was heading for trouble.

'You have been on roundabouts. At night. Explain.'

It was like the title of a creative writing essay. Sumo saved me. He coughed and stood up.

'Better be off, time for Shima's feed.'

Mum saw spatters of blood on his shirt.

'Where's your dad?' she said.

'He's not mi dad,' said Sumo. 'Never was. Never will be, an' I don't think we'll be seeing 'im again. Not ever.'

Janie's mum called asking where she was.

'Why can't I stay longer?' said Janie. 'Oh please, just this once.' But her mum wasn't happy. She wanted her to go home.

Dad offered to run her back in the car and I walked with her outside.

'Stupid parents,' said Janie. 'We need to go back to Breeze's house to see if Pogsy's there.'

'I don't think there's any chance of me sneaking out either, even if I wait till Mum and Dad have gone to bed. It'll be too late to turn up at Breeze's house and if Rorty comes with me we can't make holes in her walls when she's there. We'll just have to meet up at Leakey Close early tomorrow, eight-fifteen, is that OK?'

'It'll have to be,' said Janie.

'That is if we don't find Pogsy on the roundabout tonight.'

I fell asleep on the settee. I missed dinner completely. I knew Mum was trying to wake me but I couldn't open my eyes.

It was sometime after midnight when Dad came in. He gently shook my shoulder. He was wearing combats and a black balaclava.

'What are you doing?' I said.

'I'm coming with you,' he whispered.

'Where?'

'To the roundabout.'

# 43

Thursday. 1:40 a.m.

We left by the back door and tiptoed down the side of the house into another night. Another endless, glittering sky. We giggled like a couple of silly boys. We pressed our fingers to our lips. We took exaggerated strides and waggled our arms, pretending Mum was chasing after us.

Boxgrove Drive. Hadar Way. Little side streets. Little short cuts. Shoulder to shoulder, step by step, marching to the rasping rub of my trouser seams and the swish of Dad's waterproof.

'I should have realised,' he kept saying. 'You tried to tell me. I should have realised.'

'It's all right, Dad. It's my fault for not saying anything. I just needed time to think. I didn't want to put him in any more danger and when Janie found the scar we didn't want to believe it was you. We needed time to work out who Rorty was and what he was doing here.'

'Thanks for trusting your old dad but I still can't believe I didn't twig. Even after the hair in the shower. You did a good job of hiding him.'

'He's quite good at that himself.'

We crossed the university campus. A fine rain sprayed down. The pavements glistened under the street lights. We came to the roundabout close to Breeze's house. Maybe, this time, Pogsy would find us.

There was a fire in the tarmacked hole. We saw smoke first, then the flames. We stood at the roadside and watched.

'Where is he?' said Dad.

'Camouflaged,' I breathed.

A car swept by. Then another. We crossed over and looked about.

'This is my dad,' I said to the empty space.

We heard a scuffle. A quiet voice.

'I's here,' it said. Rorty clicked and unveiled.

I heard Dad gasp. There was disbelief and wonder in his eyes. He knelt down. He stared and stared as if he just couldn't believe what he was seeing.

'Who are you?' he whispered. 'Where have you come from?'

'I's Rorty Thrutch. I's comin from green place. Many, many greens in misty misty clouds an seas of hushness.'

'You are extraordinary,' said Dad. He reached out his hand. 'I feel enormously privileged. How do you do, Mister Rorty Thrutch? How do you jolly well do?'

We propped ourselves against the wooden flower tubs. We huddled around him in the shadows. Dad stared, trying to work him out, trying to find a place for him in the history of mankind, trying to understand how he came to be here on Planet Earth and here, in front of us, on a roundabout in the middle of Bradborough.

Rorty told some of his story. How little he remembered of being taken from his home, of Quix's lab or how he and Pogsy had escaped from it. How frightened he'd been of the cars and the lights and how, in all the confusion, he'd become separated from Pogsy. At first he'd hidden on roundabouts and then he'd found the Burrows where he'd survived on fish and roots and berries. He told us how he gradually learned to copy objects and move them. How he discovered he could paint through his fingers and how he could send and receive messages in his head. And soon after he'd found me, little memories began to return of Pogsy and the Forest and the Molimo.

'Why roundabouts?' whispered Dad.

'Because they're familiar and safe,' I said. 'Rorty's hut. His camp. His fires. His breath through the Molimo. Everything works in circles.'

Dad hung his head as if it was all too much, then looked up to the heavens as if an answer might fall from there.

'Forest is wakin,' said Rorty. 'I's knowin Molimo is searchin Pogsy an is singin high high as topsie-trees. I's knowin Pogsy is nearin.'

It was earlier than the other night. Cars kept on passing. Some slowed and paused, curious about us and about the fire. There were late-night dog walkers. There were kids traipsing about, squealing and kicking cans at each other. We needed to disappear. We needed to melt into the roundabout. We needed a billion trillion atoms to be copied in their exact shape and form and to be pasted over us.

I saw beads of sweat along the folds of Dad's brow.

'It doesn't hurt,' I told him. 'You can't feel a thing.'

'Is ready-steady?' said Rorty.

We nodded. He traced a section of the tub and the grass. He pointed at Dad and clicked. Dad vanished instantly. I saw the outline of his hands lift and turn. I saw the edges of him twitch and jiggle.

'Good God,' he kept saying. 'Good God, Kofi.'

'You have to keep still,' I said. 'Or you won't fit with the background.'

But he couldn't. He couldn't stop fidgeting and chuntering.

Rorty camouflaged me, then himself, then the fire.

'Close your eyes,' I whispered. 'And listen to the Molimo.'

I was in the Forest again. Towers of green trailing vines. Voices were calling, children were singing little melodies and I imagined I was following them. There was a circle of huts in a circle of trees. Sticks click-clacking. Yelps and whoops. Flames stretching and shivering and flecks of burning ash spinning to the sky. It was the Fire Dance. Bodies twirling, voices drumming through my bones and a blur of glowing faces moving from shadow to light, shadow to light.

I heard their voices.

*Bring them back,* they cried. *Bring them home.*

Darkness crept over the Forest. The sound of the Molimo was fading. The smell of the earth and the fire smoke slowly drifted away.

Then Dad's voice. A whisper.

'You all right, Kofi?'

'Yeah,' I said.

'I was in a forest.'

'Me too.'

'No, *really*, Kofi.'

I smiled. 'Yeah. Yeah, I know.'

Dad got to his feet.

'Hallucinating.'

'Or hypnotised.'

We looked around, hoping Pogsy was there. We searched around the flower tubs and by the roadside. I saw Rorty's dark, sad eyes.

'Pogsy not hearin us. Darkness is stayin. Pogsy Dead and Gone For Ever.'

## 44

Thursday. 8:05 a.m.

I wasn't sure if it was her at first. She'd pulled up her hood and was hunched over with her head in her hands. It was the mauve coat that I recognised. Teachers only seem to have one coat.

I was on my way to Leakey Close to meet up with Janie. But here was Breeze sitting on a wooden bench on the corner of Glaston Avenue. I could hear her sobbing. I walked over to her and stood there a while.

She glanced up.

'You look like you haven't slept,' she said, softly.

'I haven't. Well, not much.'

She took a tissue and wiped her nose. She patted the bench for me to sit down. 'Worried about something?'

she said. Little tear bulbs were gathering in the corners of her eyes. She wiped them away.

'Not as much as you are,' I said.

Her eyes flooded again.

'Here.' I passed her my pocket pack. 'Anti-viral, ultra-soft and super-absorbent.'

Breeze smiled. 'Thank you.'

She sucked in a lungful of air and blew it out again. She straightened her coat and drew herself up on the seat.

'I'm still not sure,' she said.

'About what?'

'I don't even know if I can tell you that.'

We sat a while. Birds were chirruping. Cars were swooshing along a road somewhere.

'Is the baby all right?' I asked.

Her brow crumpled as she turned to me.

'We couldn't help noticing the nappies and car seat. And we heard crying.'

Breeze's shoulders shook slightly as she giggled, then she broke down in tears again. After a while she gathered herself and drew in another shuddery breath.

'Miss Ndiaye. I need to ask you something. Have you recently bought a pair of heavy-duty bolt cutters?'

'Yes,' she said.

'For the specific use of cutting through chains on a garage door?'

She smiled. She nodded.

'To rescue Pogsy?'

'You know her name? Yes. *Yes*. I rescued her. All that chatter at school about the monkey in Sumo's garage, I knew it was her. And so *you*. It *is* you.'

I closed my eyes and felt like I was floating. 'I'm so happy,' I said. 'You can't believe how happy I am.'

She wrapped her arms around me.

'And Rorty's safe too,' I said.

'That is truly *wonderful* news.'

Breeze looked down and shook her head, her face heavy with sadness again. 'Pogsy isn't. Last night I came back from the Parent-Teacher meeting and they had gone. Pogsy and the baby. She is only four weeks old.'

Neither of us could think about going to school. We hurried up to her house, up the drive past the ancient Volvo estate.

'She must have used the spare key to unlock the front door and just walked out,' said Breeze.

We went inside. Nothing was out of place. We peeped

into Pogsy's room. There was a Moses basket and a changing mat on the floor.

'Why would she leave the safety of my house? I'm so afraid for them, Kofi. They must be in dreadful danger.'

I took out my phone. Janie was on her way, racing up Boxgrove Drive.

'I knew it was her!' she yelled. I held the phone at arm's length until she'd calmed down.

'But Pogsy and the baby went missing last night. We think they just walked out of Miss Ndiaye's house.'

Janie was quiet for a moment.

'It's the Molimo, isn't it? You were on the university roundabout last night and Pogsy must have heard it. Maybe you'd gone before she got there. I'll be outside your house in two minutes.'

I dived into the car next to Breeze. She screeched through the gears and charged through amber lights.

'Stop at my house,' I shouted. 'We need Rorty and Janie.'

We pulled up outside. Breeze got out and stood by the car. When she saw him she went down on one knee and enclosed him in her arms. They spoke quietly to each other for some moments. I knew she was telling him about the baby.

'Let's go and find them,' I said.

# 45

Thursday. 9:08 a.m.

Breeze bumped the car on to the kerb and left the lights flashing. We dashed, one by one, across the road to the university roundabout. I thought we'd find them there behind the flower tubs. It was the perfect place to hide.

'Think. Think!' yelled Janie.

'They must be on another one with trees and bushes,' I said.

'What about the massive roundabout past the hospital? There's flower beds and loads of trees. It's practically a forest.'

We piled into the car again and shot down Ashby Road.

'I jumped a red light,' said Breeze.

'Good,' said Janie.

We dumped the car. I was first to cross. There were deep shadows under the oaks and sycamores. Tall bushes in circles of lavender. Someone was moving in a dark coat. Then two more men at the edges. One was tying the strings of a large black bag.

'Quix!' I shouted.

He turned and froze. It was the first time I'd seen him look afraid.

'You're not taking them away,' I said. 'You better stop now or there'll be a war between us.'

Quix glided from beneath the trees. He was shaking his head.

'Can't stop *interfering*, can you?' He caught sight of Breeze. 'Well, finally you emerge from the gloom, Miss Ndiaye. I wondered when you'd start causing trouble.'

'It's time for you to stop, Nigel,' she said.

She walked right up to him. Quix looked beyond her to the road. He seemed uneasy but tried to hide it.

'Ah, and here's my little friend sporting a splendid tracksuit and bobble hat, accompanied by Miss Janie Watts.'

Quix shouted to the men. 'Let's get on with it. Get them in the car, Gerry. As soon as I've got this one, we're leaving.'

I charged past Quix, careered into Gerry and tried to prise the black bag from his hands. Gerry turned. He kicked me, shoved me to the ground.

'Get lost, kid. You're way out of your depth.'

I yelled.

'There's a baby in there! She's the rarest, most precious thing on this planet.'

We heard her crying and Pogsy's calm voice trying to comfort her. The younger man stood and listened.

'Jeez! They're speaking,' he said. 'Hear that, Gerry? They're speaking words. Listen mate, listen to 'em.'

Gerry let go and leaned closer.

'Giving me the creeps that is.'

'Hey, Nige, you didn't say they's talking animals.'

Quix strode over. 'Isn't that the whole point of this? What do you think Operation Silent Talk is all about? I haven't time for this. Get out of my way.'

Quix started to drag the black bag towards a van parked on the kerb. We heard them wailing. We heard Pogsy calling for us.

A dark storm surged inside me. I ran straight for Quix and bulldozed his feet. Breeze and Janie quickly followed and toppled him to the ground.

Quix yelled. 'Tom! Gerry! Get the other one and get that damn bag in the van. I'm doubling your wages.'

Gerry loped over and swung the bag on his shoulder but from the cover of the trees Rorty was already raising his hands.

Quix was on his back pinned down by Breeze and Janie but he was able to slide a small device from his pocket. He pressed a switch and lay there grinning at us.

'Off you go then,' he said. 'Show us what you can do, Mr Thrutch. Let's see MINDLINK at its best. Show us the cleverness of its inventor.'

Rorty widened his hands. He was trying to separate Gerry from the black bag but it seemed like nothing was happening.

Quix laughed. 'Electromagnetic interference,' he spluttered. 'Clever old Dad didn't figure that one out, did he?' He yelled louder, 'Grab the other one, Tom, and get them out of here.'

Tears seeped from Breeze's eyes. Janie turned to me and glared. I shook my head.

'It could interfere with MINDLINK. It could stop it working but I'm sure Dad must have thought of that.'

We heard whimpering and little cries. Quix tried once more to get up but Janie got hold of his shoulders and Breeze raised her fist.

Tom was heading for Rorty in the shadows. He slowed as he approached. Rorty looked down the line of his right arm, then his left. He trained an index finger on Gerry and the other on Tom. I could see the concentration on his face. The desperation in his dark eyes.

Tom twitched violently. At the same time I saw the jolt in Gerry's body. There was shock on their faces as they realised they could no longer move. Gerry hit the ground hard. He clung to the bag but Rorty kept tugging, shifting him closer. Tom skidded. He squatted to keep his balance. He glided along like he was skiing on grass.

I grabbed the box from Quix's hand and slipped it into my pocket. 'Electromagnetic what?' I said. 'You underestimate my dad. Big time.'

I ran to Gerry and tugged the bag from his grip. He was shaking, a look of pure terror on his face. Tom had collapsed beside him.

'When he releases you, you'd better run for it,' I said. 'And take Quix with you.'

I watched them stagger to their feet. They dragged Quix upright and escorted him to the van.

Someone yelled from a passing car.

'Need any help? You all right?'

'All fine,' I called. 'It's Professor Nigel Quix. He's blind drunk.'

'This early?' The man in the car laughed and waved and rejoined the morning traffic.

# 46

Thursday. 9:33 a.m.

Under the trees, Rorty kneeled.

He opened the black bag.

He leaned towards the two little figures and stayed a while, just gazing. Then they pressed their heads together and clung to each other for what seemed like an eternity.

The baby cried.

She emerged from between them. A little bundle. Impossibly small. Perfectly formed. We gathered round her and stared and smiled. I glanced over at Breeze and saw her eyes glistening.

We lifted them into Breeze's car. We took out the parcel shelf and flipped up the spare seats and strapped the baby into the car seat.

Pogsy Blue had a sweet face and kind eyes. Her hair was in tufts and curls like Rorty's. I peered at them and gazed and wondered and realised that we are not so alone on this amazing planet of ours. Another evolutionary path. Another species of human that must be protected and kept secret.

'You all right back there?' said Breeze.

'Fine,' we said. 'Everything's just fine.'

# 47

Friday. 9:17 a.m.

We woke around nine. I heard Dad leaving for work and the baby crying. Mum was already in the spare room with her medical bag. Pogsy was holding the baby and Rorty was telling her what Mum was doing. It was strange to hear them speaking their own language. There are clicks and hums between the words.

Sumo had come over. He'd made us a tray of tea and juice and piles of jammy toast. He stood a while just listening.

'Can't understand a word of that,' he said. 'But she's not speaking English coz she doesn't have MINDLINK, does she?'

'That's right,' I said.

Sumo grinned. 'I like her sort of speaking better,' he said. 'Called school, by the way. Told them we'd be there this afternoon. Said we were doing last-minute Origins stuff. I said it was all right with Breeze.'

'Thanks.' I smiled.

Janie came in. We sat on the floor quietly gazing at the new arrivals.

'I just can't believe we've found her,' said Janie, softly. 'I can't believe she's really here.'

Mum said the baby was fit and healthy and the new mum was doing well.

'Can I hold her?' asked Janie.

She was wrapped in my old baby blanket. Janie cradled her and gazed at her beautiful face.

Pogsy said something. She looked at us.

'Pogsy sayin thankin you,' said Rorty. 'Is sayin safe now. Is sayin Darkness Dead an Gone For Ever. Is thankin oldens an spirit voices an Forest.'

The baby started to cry. Janie couldn't calm her. Sumo scooped her up and walked her round the room. He talked. He sang to her.

'What y'gonna call her?' he asked.

Rorty turned and gazed at the sky out of the window.

It was white with a few smudges of grey. He clicked and hummed.

'All overs an everywheres is wafts an whiffy winds. Is bringin Great Blue an is bringin Great Dark. Is shakin Forest greens an makin wheezie trees. Is blowin KingWings to mountain moons. An in hushness, is bringin huntin threads that we's sniffin. In zippy days, whiffy winds is dancin. In dozy days, whiffy winds is sleepin. An Rorty's breathins is blowin Molimo all curlin an sky-loopy-twistin on blusty-flows searchin Pogsy. An Forest stirs. An Forest smiles, an is blowin life breath, an baby's huffypuffs is shiverin an shakin an tumblin out an is windin coddle-twines round Pogsy Blue. An wen baby is cryin an Pogsy is cryin, Great Blue is paintin colourins, is makin smilin agen.'

Rorty opened his arms. He gazed at his little daughter.

'We's thankin Forest. Is father an mother. Is givin bountifuls. Is givin teeny-tinies. Is givin big-bigger-biggies. Forest is carein us. We's thankin Forest. Is returnin Pogsy an baby.'

'So what y'gonna call her?' Sumo said softly.

'Is namin Nama Dom.'

'How lovely,' said Janie. 'What does it mean?'

'Is meanin Rainbow,' said Rorty.

*

295

Later that afternoon, we left Rorty, Pogsy and Nama Dom with Mum and set off for school. Our class was in the hall pinning up posters and arranging things on tables. Breeze stood tall and proud in a sunshine-yellow dress. She beckoned me over.

'Detective Darwin,' she whispered.

'Sorry we're late. There were all sorts of things to sort out . . .'

She held my gaze for a while. She pressed her lips together to stop herself from smiling.

'Presentation ready?'

'Just about,' I said.

We wandered over to the back of the hall. Janie was moving photos from Dawn W's display and Dawn W was trying to stick them on again.

'You're taking up *far* too much space,' said Janie. 'You only need *one* grinning Dawn and *one* grinning Marilyn, not six of each.'

Breeze stepped in. She wheeled over another board to make room for them both. Janie's was all about genes for red hair. She'd ditched the idea about her mum's ancestors. The bone she'd found in the field was from a sheep.

'Happy?' said Breeze.

'I am now,' said Janie.

Spread over the rest of the display boards were super-sized photographs of the Jameson twins' fingerprints, Jez's family photos pointing out similar noses, eyes and chins and Jocelyn's model of DNA which stretched over five metres.

Hammer was wielding a Viking spear he'd bought on eBay.

'Here y'are, Stealth,' he said. 'Brought y'this.' He handed him an A3 printout.

'What is it?' said Stealth.

'Your origins, mate. Cyanobacteria. First life forms. Three an'half billion years old.'

'Older than everyone else's stuff?'

'By flipping miles.'

'Cheers,' he said.

The end-of-school bell sounded. We left the display complete and ready for Monday morning's assembly. Sumo wanted to read out his letters but Breeze said he'd have everyone in tears.

'When I find him,' said Sumo, 'he's going to come and live with us. He's going to be Shima's dad and my dad. And I'm going to change mi name to Sebastien Suparman. Awesome that is. I could be a film star with a name like that. What d'you think?'

# 48

Friday. 8:46 p.m.

The curtains were closed. The lights had been dimmed. We moved about carefully and talked in whispers. The Molimo was singing softly. We could all feel it. It seeped into us. It melted us inside.

Cradled in the deep wings of the armchair, Pogsy slept with Nama Dom. Mum draped a blanket over them. She stood a while and gazed. She whispered and shook her head.

'What a miracle. What a marvel they both are.'

Janie was by the fire. Her eyes were closed. I wondered what the Molimo was conjuring for her. I was there, with her, inside that same moment. At the heart of the Forest, hearing the Forest rejoicing.

The doorbell rang.

'I'll get it,' I said.

Sumo hung up his jacket and slipped off his shoes. He straightened them on the mat.

We gathered in the lounge. We talked in low voices. Mum, Dad and Sumo on the sofa. Me, Janie and Rorty on the floor.

'I don't know why people can't be nice to each other,' said Janie. 'All of this is because people can't be nice.'

Mum shrugged. 'It's human nature. Nasty was useful once. It meant survival rather than certain death. Now it's all greed and ambition.'

'Professor Quix is a greedy man,' said Dad. 'He took you from your home, Rorty. You and Pogsy. Professor Quix took you both from your Forest. Kofi helped you and hid you, and with Janie and Sumo, tried to protect you. And you helped yourself by learning to use MINDLINK in ways we could never have imagined. But if people get to know about you, you'd cause a sensation across this world. Scientists would want to study you and measure you and take samples from you. You would be more important than the first men who landed on the moon.'

'Way more,' said Janie.

'Moon?' said Rorty. He pointed to the sky.

'Yes. Three men flew a rocket to the moon.'

Rorty's eyes danced. He chuckled and slapped his sides. We couldn't help smiling with him.

'Do you want to go back home?' said Dad. 'You and Pogsy and Nama Dom?'

I looked at Rorty. I felt a sudden heaviness inside.

'You'd be safe on Heron's Island,' said Janie. 'It would be lovely. We could come and visit and I could babysit.'

Dad shook his head. 'Think about it. If they stay here, they'd be forever in hiding. Do you think us *Homo sapiens* would leave them alone once the world found out about them? They must be protected. They need to be back in their own environment. In the Forest.'

'So tell us what *you* want to do, Rorty,' I said.

Rorty pondered. 'Quixie gone now?' he asked.

'Yes,' said Dad. 'Disappeared without a trace.'

'I didn't know that,' I said.

'The laboratory has been cleared out. Apparently he's left his wife and son.'

'Poor Jon,' said Janie.

'What was he gonna do with 'im anyway?' said Sumo. 'What's the point of them MINDLINKs?'

'Quix said they were developing technologies vital to the security of the world,' I said, 'essential to the future of our planet. But by that he meant implanting it in soldiers so they'd have mind-to-mind communication, or selling it to terrorists. And now he knows what MINDLINK can do in Rorty's brain, the possibilities are terrifying.'

'I can't believe anyone would be so evil,' said Mum.

'What do you think, Rorty?' I turned to him. 'Do you want to go home? Do you and Pogsy and Nama Dom want to go back to the Forest?'

Rorty looked at each of us with his deep, brown, smiling eyes. He didn't need to say what he was thinking.

Tears trickled down Janie's face. She dabbed them with her sleeve.

'It's for the best,' she said. 'I know it is. But we're really going to miss you.'

She began to sob and I felt my throat tighten and my heart pattering.

'There's just one problem,' I said. 'We don't know where home is.'

# 49

The assembly hall was packed. Younger classes were on the floor, the older ones on chairs.

Jocelyn went first. She asked some of the little ones to hold up her gigantic model of DNA. She told us that all animals and plants have a common ancestor that lived one point six billion years ago.

'We share thirty-six per cent of our genes with fruit flies, sixty-five per cent with chickens and ninety-eight per cent with chimpanzees,' she said. 'Does anyone know how much of our DNA we share with bananas?'

There were squeaks of laughter.

'A surprising fifty per cent,' Jocelyn announced.

'How much do we share with dinosaurs?' someone asked.

Heads turned to Velociraptor, who was nodding off in a corner.

'Actually that question cannot be answered precisely,' said Jocelyn, 'because no dinosaur DNA has survived. But I think it's important that we all know that DNA is very similar for all human beings. You share ninety-nine point nine per cent with whoever you're sitting next to, wherever they're from and whatever they look like. We're all pretty much the same.'

There were cheers and everyone clapped. Then it was Hammer's turn.

He strode up to the front in full Viking costume. He told us his surname 'Carr' meant that his ancestors were from Shetland and Scandinavia. He bumbled on about genes for fighting and maiming. The mock battle got a bit out of hand and Erik Bloodaxe (Hammer) and Thorfinn Skullsplitter (Stealth) had to be prised apart by Mr Steele.

After Hammer it was Janie. Breeze helped her wheel her display board to the front.

'Good morning, everyone,' said Janie. 'As part of our project on Origins, I'm going to talk about how we inherit red or ginger hair.'

There were photos of her family going back through generations. There was a map of how the genes had been passed down.

She asked us to name a famous redhead.

'Prince Harry,' said one of the sixth-form girls.

'Erik the Red,' shouted Hammer.

'Amy Pond,' said someone from the Doctor Who club.

'Brilliant examples,' said Janie.

She traced the redhead gene through her family. She explained how her ginger-haired brother must have two genes and she has just one.

'However,' said Janie, 'if I married Ron Weasley, which by the way I fully intend to do, we'd have a fifty per cent chance of having a child with red hair.'

Everyone laughed and applauded as Janie sat down again.

Then Breeze turned to me. I walked to the front. I was thinking of Rorty and where he'd come from. I thought how amazed everyone would be if they knew. I looked out at the sea of faces.

'There are six billion humans on our planet,' I said. 'And from where I'm standing it looks like most of you are here.'

I heard Mr Steele's chuckle over the noise.

'As Jocelyn said, all six billion of us are very close relatives. But DNA doesn't just tell us how closely related we are, it also gives us clues as to where the first humans came from. And this is where we think it began.'

Breeze wheeled in my map of the world. I'd drawn lines from Ethiopia that stretched over Europe, China, South America and Australia.

'The oldest human fossils have been found here in East Africa.' I pointed to the map. 'Scientists are pretty sure that about fifty thousand years ago, our African ancestors left this region to walk across the world.'

I strode across the width of the hall and back again.

'It must have taken a very long time,' I said. 'Special bits of DNA called markers found in people today can be used to trace where we came from and where we migrated to. These markers show that during one of the ice ages, when continents were closer together, some humans walked along the coast from Africa to Australia, and others crossed an ice bridge from Europe to North America.'

I traced the routes over the continents.

'Of course, today, none of those ancient human species are still alive. We are all *Homo sapiens*.' I scanned the room. 'At least I think most of us are. But sometimes I wonder. How do we know for sure? Maybe there is another species of human tucked away in a remote corner of the planet. And what would we do if we found them?'

There was a pause before I took a bow, then I walked back to my seat as the applause subsided.

Mr Steele stepped forward. He mouthed something but no one took any notice. His voice was lost in the clapping and whistling. He waved the noise down.

'Electrifying presentations from Miss Ndiaye's class,' he said. 'Fascinating DNA facts from Jocelyn. A wonderfully interactive portrayal of our Scandinavian relatives by Eric Bloodaxe. Thank you to Janie for an insight into the inheritance of red hair and to Kofi – what a way to set our minds wondering if we really are the only humans on the planet. I thank everyone for a brilliant assembly. Thank you.'

There was rumbling and chattering as the teachers moved out of the hall. Rows of students followed. A few came to peer at the displays and to wield Hammer's Viking spear.

Breeze thanked Jocelyn. She thanked Janie and Hammer. She asked Sumo if he'd heard anything. He shook his head and smiled.

'Off to your lessons now.' She clapped as if we were small children. 'Don't leave anything valuable behind.'

She turned to me. 'That just leaves your astonishing story.'

'I'd love to hear yours,' I said. I watched her. There was a glimmer in her eyes. 'My story,' I said, 'would have to include the bit about how Detective Darwin saved you from the sniffer dogs. And yours would have to explain how you happen to know about two ancient hominins.'

'Three,' she said. She smiled.

'Miss Ndiaye. We have to take them home.'

She nodded slowly. She moved closer and whispered, 'Latitude: -1.473121. Longitude: 5.642424. Off you go now. You'll be late for your lesson.'

# 50

It was near the Gulf of Guinea. A tiny island in a topaz sea. Too tiny to see on Google Earth and oddly circular, according to Breeze. She came round that evening. We gathered in the lounge saying how extraordinary this all was. How mind-blowing. How unbelievable.

Breeze had studied science in New York and palaeoanthropology in London. Quix had contacted her after her expedition to Ethiopia. He needed her expertise on a trip to a remote island. She thought they were going to excavate skulls. She was expecting to be sifting for stone flakes and vertebrae.

'I was amazed and horrified,' said Breeze. 'They shot them with tranquilliser darts. They put them in crates and brought them over here on a cargo plane. Professor

Quix threatened us to keep quiet about it or we'd feel the full force of the authorities upon us.'

'Why bring them here?' I said.

'Because of your dad,' she explained. 'But I couldn't let them get away with it. So I followed them here, managed to get a teaching job and started the search.'

Things happened quickly after that. Our dining room was turned into a Command Centre, like the White House Situation Room, except smaller and minus the patriotic flags. There were phones and laptops, printouts of shipping timetables, a world map with a red circle around the island's coordinates. Mum and Janie were in charge of travel provisions – clothes, nappies, blankets and vaccinations. Dad said I should look into solar-powered internet. Sumo was singing softly to Shima and Nama Dom.

Breeze found an airfreight courier service capable of moving animals, regardless of species or location. The plan was to fly them to Gabon then take a boat from Port-Gentil to the island. Back to their home.

'Perfect,' she said. 'I'll travel with them. I brought them here. I'd be honoured to take them back. We just have to work out how to get them through customs and veterinary clearance.'

'How did it work last time?' asked Dad.

'Private aircraft,' said Breeze. 'I have no idea who organised it.'

'We have a secret to share with you.' I turned to her. 'It's the final part of the Astonishing Story.'

'Let's have a nice brew first,' said Mum. 'Are you easily shocked, Miss Ndiaye?'

It probably wasn't necessary that Breeze was sitting down when Rorty camouflaged, but we took the precaution anyway. At the moment of his disappearance, her lips remained pursed and her eyes unmoving for several seconds.

Then she said, 'I see, or rather I don't.'

And we all laughed.

'That's the best reaction ever,' said Janie. 'First time he did that, I almost fainted.'

Dad went into a long spiel about the MINDLINK programme and how it turns thought into action and about decoders and prosthetics and restoring mobility. Then the mystery of how the chips in Rorty's brain replicate matter.

'Replicate?' said Breeze.

'My next research project,' said Dad. 'To work out how that's possible.'

The plan was to transport Rorty, Pogsy and Nama Dom in a container with some exotic animals. Breeze had contacts at London zoo. They'd remain camouflaged until they reached the island. Until it was time to say goodbye.

'Will they be safe?' said Janie. 'What if Quix goes back?'

Dad smiled. 'I think Rorty knows what to do if that happens.'

'Talking of deleting things,' I said. 'What are we going to do about Col?'

'What happened to him?' said Breeze.

'He sort of disappeared.'

'You said deleted.'

'Yes. Another of Rorty's many talents. But don't worry. Rorty can restore him.'

'I's bringing back baddy-bad?' said Rorty.

'We have to,' I said. 'But we'll make sure he doesn't bother you again. I promise.'

'He could live in Port-Gentil,' suggested Breeze. 'It's not a bad place. There's work. He'll have a home. I'll ask my friends to keep an eye on him.'

\*

We were exhausted. Sumo had gone. Janie was asleep on the floor. Breeze gathered up her coat and bag. We stepped outside, just the two of us, and breathed the night air.

'I'll walk back with you if you like,' I said.

We strolled down Boxgrove Drive.

'I'd like you to tell me about the island. Every single detail. Everything you can remember.'

'Yes, Kofi,' said Breeze. 'I'd like that too.'

# 51

Sunday was our last day. It had arrived so quickly. All the packing was done. All the preparations had been made. We didn't know what to do with ourselves until Janie said:

'Beach.'

We all turned and looked at her. Even little Nama Dom.

'Let's go to the sea,' she said, 'for today we need to be with the sand and the wind and the waves. All of us. Together.'

So we went.

We put our bikes on the train. Pogsy was hidden in my rucksack, Rorty in Sumo's and Nama Dom in Janie's. We got off at Sandyworth Station and cycled the last bit. We tore down thin grey roads, past giant hedges and stone houses. The verges were a blur of whites and pinks and yellows. The wind roared in our ears, snatched our breath away. Janie threw out her legs and screamed with the thrill of it all.

'Nearly there!' we shouted.

We turned into a sandy lane and caught the salty smell of the sea. We followed a signpost for Dilly Cove. At the end we pushed our bikes down a grassy slope and dodged sheep droppings and stamped our way through forests of bracken. We stopped at the cliff edge. There was no one in sight. Not a soul on the beach. We put down the rucksacks and our little family clambered out, Rorty in corduroys and a woolly hat, Pogsy in a thick cardigan and shorts and Nama Dom wrapped in a blanket. We stood there together, two boys, a girl and three little hominins, staring out at the glittering sea.

We left the bikes and followed a winding path down the cliffs. The tide was out. The sand lay before us, cold and steely grey.

'First to the sea!' called Janie. She set off over the rocks.

I scrambled after her, felt my feet sinking into the sand. I ran full pelt trying to match her footprints.

'You'll never catch me,' she yelled. 'You're rubbish at running!'

She plunged into the water. Waves crashed around her. She leapt back, arms reeling, yelling into the vastness around her.

'I love you, sand and sea and wind. I LOVE YOOOOOOU!'

Her trainers were drenched. Her hair fell in raggedy strands around her face.

'Crackers, that's what you are, Janie Watts,' I said.


We ate cheese and lettuce sandwiches. We sipped Diet Coke. Crunched our way through a family bag of crisps. Sumo wrapped his coat around Pogsy and Nama Dom and sheltered them from the wind. Rorty spun Olioze around his fingers. He watched the waves rolling in.

'Is fishies in sparklie sea. Big juicy meaties an tiddlie-tinies.'

'Did you live near the sea?' said Sumo.

'Is long sticky walkin day an steppin down-down an buzzi-buzzin all the ways an climbin down-down an smellin wafty freshness an seein blusie-blues all over an around.'

'How could Quix have taken you away from all that loveliness?' said Janie.

I closed my eyes and breathed. 'I have a question for you, Sebastien Fitzgerald and Rorty Thrutch and Janie Watts. It's a "what" question.'

Janie giggled. 'Go on then with your "what" question.'

'If you could choose anything from your wildest dreams, *what* would it be?'

'Oh I know that,' said Sumo. He sat forward and clasped his hands. 'It'd be finding mi dad and having 'im come and live with us at home, so mi mam would have someone who loved 'er and treated 'er proper, and Shima would 'ave someone who'd play with 'er and make her laugh and I'd 'ave a proper dad . . . who loved me.'

'I think I might know how to find him and if I don't, I know someone who can help,' I said.

'Really?' said Sumo.

'Yes,' I said.

Sumo's eyes shone. 'You're a real mate, d'you know that?'

'So are you,' I said.

I turned to Rorty. 'I think we already know what you would choose.'

'Is Pogsy. Is Nama Dom. Is Kofi, is Janie, is Sumo. Is all stayin. Is all goin home. Is all in wildy dreams.'

I felt my throat tightening and tears gathering. 'I know we can't all be together and soon we'll be very far away from each other but because of MINDLINK we can stay connected. We'll be able to talk to you and send pictures and make sure you're safe.'

Rorty came to sit on my lap and wrapped his arms around me. I couldn't hold back any longer. Tears filled my eyes and spilled down my cheeks and Rorty gently wiped them away.

'Your turn, Janie,' I whispered.

She sighed and stared out at the sea.

'Wildest?' she said.

I nodded.

'Completely and utterly barmiest?'

'As barmy as you like,' I said.

'I'd want to fly. First I'd run like mad feeling the air rushing past, then I'd rise and I'd be gliding, not flapping, just laid out bang-flat in the air looking down at the roof tops and the miniature gardens and strings of teenie-weenie cars. And I'd see fields, strips of yellow, green and rusty brown like a crazy collage, and ploughed fields like you've dragged a fork through chocolate fudge, and rivers like strips of sparkling metal.'

She rubbed her hands. Her eyes were shining. 'That's what's in my wildest and completely barmiest dreams.'

'Be careful what you wish for,' I said.


The tide had turned. The frothy waters surged and fell away. Seagulls plunged from the cliffs, screeched over our heads. We looked out at the marks we'd made in the sand.

'I don't get it. How's it going to work?' she said.

'Wait. Trust me,' I said.

She jumped up and down. She banged her hands together. She couldn't stop grinning. 'What if someone sees?' she squealed.

The cliffs loomed behind us, great shoulders of rock tapering down to the pools and the sea below.

'This is Dilly Cove,' I said. 'No one's going to see us here.'

Rorty stood next to me. His eyes were twinkling. Janie eased off her trainers and stripped off her socks. She caught me looking.

'Less weight,' she said.

'Start from over there,' I told her. 'I'll say when to go then run parallel to the sea.'

Before she took her position, she slipped off her jacket and flung it behind her.

'More less weight,' she yelled, grinning.

She placed one foot on the line and leaned forward, her eyes fixed ahead.

'Ready?' I said to Rorty.

'I's ready-steady,' he said.

Janie was still.

Poised.

Waiting.

*This is it*, I thought. I cupped my hands round my mouth.

'OK, Janie. Go!'

She surged forward, arms pumping the air, feet pounding the sand. She ran tall and erect. Her jeans flapped. Her skimpy top twisted and writhed. Her hair streamed behind her.

Rorty stretched out his hand and closed one eye. He looked down the line of his arm and trained his index finger upon her. His hand twitched. She felt it too. She slowed, glanced over, then Rorty raised his arm and Janie lifted into the air.

A few feet from the ground and still moving forward, her head was bowed against the wind. She flew higher over rocks and rock pools, dark clumps of seaweed, gulleys and rivulets carved into the sand. The wind blew and buffeted her. Rorty swung her round, following the curve of the cliffs. Even from that distance we could hear her screaming. Soon she was head-on coming back towards us, over the rocks, over the sand again.

'Put me down!' she squealed. 'Put me down!'

Rorty lowered her gently. Her feet found the earth and she yelped and flapped her hands. She staggered towards us like a mad thing. Hugged us and kissed us. Her face was wet and icy cold. She bent over, rested her hands on her thighs, blew out, stood up again.

'What about that?' she said. 'Can you believe it? I was flying. Flying I tell ya!'

Sumo came running over with Pogsy and Nama Dom.

'That's mad!' he shouted. 'I thought I'd seen everything what with green paint and shrinking helicopters, but that's the maddest of 'em all!'

Janie wanted to go again. She wanted to swoop this time. Loop the loop. Do a Lancaster roll. A kite loop and twist. She practised the manoeuvres over the wet sand.

The gulls circled. The waves edged closer. The farthest rocks were dark pinnacles in the swirling sea.

'What about it, Rorty?' I said.

'I's doin two.'

'Both of us? Are you sure?'

'I's doin two,' he said again.

Janie grabbed my hand. 'Come on. Let's go!'

'But I'm allergic to kite loop twists . . .' I shouted.

Janie took hold of my arm and hauled me to the starting line.

'And absolutely no . . .'

She slapped a hand across my mouth.

'And he absolutely adores loop the loops,' she said, and we got into position.

We paused, one in front of the other. We started to run, little steps at first so we'd stay close, then a surge and a strange tingling and tugging as feet parted from sand. I gasped and hung limp as I watched the great arch of the cove open up and the black bands of rock and silvery sea below.

Then Janie's voice: 'Straighten out! You're supposed to be flying, y'great dodo!'

We slowed as we hugged the ragged edges of the cliffs. Tufts of spiky grass tickled our outstretched hands. We rose again, over crags, over sea pinks and yellow vetch, over lichen-speckled rocks. Janie glided ahead, hair streaming behind her.

'I love this!' she cried.

'I'm not sure I do!' I shouted.

We curved back over the beach. Lower this time. Low enough to see Rorty's outstretched hands sweep us over his head then flick us on to our sides as we glided past him. We felt spray on our faces, tasted salt on our tongues. The sea roiled around the rocks in great curling lathers of frosty white and ice blue.

I yelled, 'That's enough for me now, Rorty!' and he lowered us gently on to the sand.

It took us a while to stop laughing at the madness of it all. Sumo was the worst. Every time we caught his eye he'd collapse on the sand again with tears rolling down his cheeks. Above us, the clouds were gathering. There were spots of rain and we went to sit in the shelter of the rocks. The wind rushed up the cliff face, catapulting gulls to their nests.

'What are Pogsy's dreams?' said Janie.

Rorty turned to Pogsy and spoke quietly in their strange, ancient language with clicks and hums between the words. They touched noses, then Rorty said:

'Pogsy wantin home now.'

# 52

Janie and I were in the lounge sitting in exactly the same place as we were eleven weeks ago, when we'd munched carrot cake and slurped smoothies and wondered what on earth I'd seen on the Tesco roundabout.

I wished it were then, now.

Now, there was a truck outside and in the truck was a wooden crate with four small perspex windows. Now, there was Mum and Dad toing and froing with suitcases and checklists and last-minute paperwork. Now, there were three extraordinary little hominins huddled beside us ready to start their journey back home.

Breeze stood in the doorway.

'It's time,' she said.

We kneeled next to Rorty, Pogsy and Nama Dom and enclosed them in our arms. We pushed our heads together and cried.

'We'll never, ever forget you,' I whispered.

'I's keepin head pictures all the days,' said Rorty.

Pogsy tied little bracelets around our wrists and we took turns to kiss Nama Dom goodbye.

A burst of sunshine filled the room and we got to our feet and walked hand in hand out of the front door to the truck.

I looked deep into Rorty's eyes. I felt my eyes filling again and a huge surge of sadness bubbling inside.

'I'll miss you so much,' I said. I bent down to hold him again. 'And I feel so privileged to have been able to help you. I hope this isn't the last time, Rorty and, anyway, somehow I have a feeling that we'll see each other again.'

'I's not feelin,' said Rorty. 'I's knowin.'

We hugged them one last time before Dad lifted them into the crate and swung the truck doors closed.

# 53

Two weeks later, I was in town. Pavements shone, wet from the rain. Sounds were muffled. An iron-grey sky hung and everything beneath it stood still and silent and sombre, like the world was holding its breath.

I was watching shoppers loping along. Kids meandering. I turned into the arcade. I passed a sign by a replacement window stall: 'Hello. Your contact today is Mike.'

Mike had no idea. The girl with eyeliner and smartphone had no idea. None of them had any idea that on a tiny island, far out in the South Atlantic Ocean, there was another human species, sharing the air that we breathe, watching the same skies burst open with rain, feeling hunger and joy and sadness, and observing the great chasm of the night with the same wonder as we do.

I went to the bookshop café. Level two. Leather chair by the window.

'All right?' said a voice.

I looked up.

'Yeah. Fine,' I said.

Janie held out her hand to show me the bracelet. I did the same. We smiled at the baby teeth, the tiny feathers, the tiny shells from Pentle Bay beach.

My phone buzzed. I opened the message.

'They're having fish and chips for tea. And a Magnum for afters.'

'It is astonishing, isn't it?' said Janie.

'Yeah,' I said. 'Pretty much.'

# Acknowledgements

Sincere thanks to Cornerstones for providing the boost I needed to believe in myself, and to Amy Waite who was the first to fall in love with Rorty.

I am grateful to my star agent, Hellie Ogden, and my scintillating editor, Sarah Lambert, for guiding me through this journey with skill, knowledge and boundless energy.

And finally, to Kofi, Janie and Rorty, who I imagined one day, sitting by my side, encouraging me to finish their story.